THE FANATICS

By the same author

The Hunters
The Liars

THE FANATICS

Peter Hill

CHARLES SCRIBNER'S SONS
New York

First U.S. edition published by Charles Scribner's Sons, 1978

Library of Congress Catalog Card Number 78–53482

ISBN 0–684–15821–3

1 3 5 7 9 11 13 15 17 19 I/C 20 18 16 14 12 10 8 6 4 2

Printed in Great Britain

TUESDAY

1 It was 7 a.m.

A woman police officer walked along Victoria Street in the direction of Parliament Square.

In her left hand she carried a smart black briefcase and under her left arm a large brown manilla envelope which bore the crest of Her Majesty's Stationery Office. On the envelope, in bold capitals, were written the words: 'Commander "A" Department. N.S.Y.'

The briefcase was heavier than it looked but she made light of it.

The police uniform suited the girl's slim figure and she drew admiring glances from passing drivers.

Checking the time by her wrist-watch, she increased her pace slightly, crossing Victoria Street at the junction with Broadway and walking along the front of the modern office building that housed New Scotland Yard.

An elderly uniformed officer stood on guard outside the plate-glass doors of the main entrance. The W.P.C. smiled at him as she approached. He pushed back the heavy glass door, held it open for her. His smile of greeting managed to be both lecherous and avuncular.

'Beautiful morning, my dear,' he said.

'Isn't it,' she replied, and rewarded him with a dazzling smile.

Another uniformed officer sat behind a large reception desk in the foyer opposite the entrance doors. He looked up as she entered.

'You're about early,' he said.

She switched on the smile again.

'Nights,' she said, 'I'm on overtime now.'

She walked diagonally to her right across the foyer, stopped in front of the bank of lifts and put the briefcase down for a moment to press the call button.

She was out of sight of the officer behind the reception desk now, hidden from his view by the left-hand wall of the recess that housed the lifts. The officer on the door, however, had entered the foyer and was watching her appreciatively.

'If you want "A" Department, it's quicker to use the other lifts,' he called out to her.

Her stomach twisted into a knot. Why didn't the stupid old bastard mind his own business? The lift arrived and the doors opened. She picked up the briefcase and stepped inside.

'I prefer the scenic route,' she called back, and stuck her tongue out at him impudently.

The officer laughed as the lift doors closed on the girl. His colleague behind the reception desk leaned forward, trying to see what was going on.

'Watch him, Miss,' he called out. 'He's a dirty old man.'

The officer on the door made an obscene gesture and returned to his post on the door.

The officer at the desk made an entry in the Arrivals Book. He wrote: '7.03 a.m. W.P.C. 518 "C" Division. For Commander "A".'

The girl had selected the third floor. She stepped out into a long, neon-lit corridor with wood-grained doors set at regular intervals in pale green walls. To her left the corridor ended with a facing door marked 'B.12'. In front of this door an elderly woman wearing a green check pinafore was operating an electric floor polisher. The cleaner continued with her work, ignoring the uniformed figure that emerged from the lift.

The girl turned right and walked purposefully towards the far end of the corridor. Halfway down she came to the entrance of another identical corridor on her right and she calculated that this would take her towards the rear of the building. She turned into this corridor and near the end she found what she was looking for, two adjacent doors marked 'Men' and 'Women'.

She walked on, mapping the maze of corridors in her mind as best she could. It took her two minutes to locate the bank of lifts that served the rear of the building, then she retraced her steps and entered the women's toilet.

The cubicles were separated by solid walls that stopped about four feet short of the ceiling. There was a similar gap above the wooden doors. The room was empty.

The girl entered the second cubicle along and locked the door. She lowered the toilet seat cover, placed the briefcase on it and opened it. She took out a large brown manilla envelope similar to the one she had carried into the building under her arm. This one was marked 'Chief Superintendent. "C" Division'.

A graffiti artist had been at work on the wall facing her. This female wit had written: 'Peter Pan was a fairy.' The girl read it, but did not find it in the least amusing. She had other things on her mind.

She placed the envelope addressed to 'Commander "A" Department' into the briefcase, and remained bent over the briefcase for a moment, both hands inside it. Then, placing one foot carefully on the toilet seat, she climbed over the cubicle door and dropped down the outside.

A second was taken checking her appearance in a wall mirror above one of the handbasins, then she walked back into the corridor and headed towards the rear bank of lifts.

It was 7.12 a.m. when she crossed the foyer towards the rear exit of the building. She waved the brown envelope casually in the direction of the officers at the reception desk and pushed her way out of the revolving door. A young C.I.D. officer nodded and grinned at her as she crossed the brief forecourt at the rear of the building.

She turned right along Broadway, then right again along Tothill Street. She had been calm throughout, but now, after it was all over, her heart was racing. It had been so easy, so *bloody* easy!

She crossed Victoria Street under the shadow of Westminster Abbey, walked with unobtrusive speed down Great Smith Street, turned right into Great Peter Street and left into Monck Street.

A small saloon car with tinted windows was parked against the kerb. She got into the front passenger seat.

'Well?'

She closed her eyes, and forced herself to relax before opening them again to look at him. His tanned-brown face was creased with worry lines, his knuckles showed white where he gripped the steering wheel.

'It was easy, like taking candy from kids,' she said.

'Yeah?'

She was suddenly irritable.

'I said so, didn't I?'

'Okay, okay.'

He noticed that a vein in her neck was pulsating fast.

'How long?' he asked.

She looked at her watch.

'Three minutes. I'd better get changed.'

She reached behind her on to the rear seat and took one of the three holdalls, placed it on the floor between her legs and began to undress.

He tried not to make his observation of her too obvious, but in the close confines of the car it was difficult. She stripped rapidly down to her briefs and it seemed to him that she delayed covering herself for a little longer than was strictly necessary. He had no objections to that. His eyes hovered over her body and he felt an unprofessional stir of desire in his stomach.

She dressed in a loose floppy sweater, a pair of faded, paint-splashed jeans and Scholl sandals. She removed the blonde wig and her own long dark hair fell about her shoulders. She wiped the modest make-up she had thought suitable for a woman police officer from her face with a tissue and then there was no longer the slightest resemblance between the neat and rather prim W.P.C. she had been and the bra-less, trendy student she now was.

She stuffed the manilla envelope and the discarded uniform into the holdall and replaced it on the rear seat.

They sat in silence.

Seconds later the bomb she had planted in New Scotland Yard exploded with a dull roar, barely muted by distance, followed by the unmistakable sound of shattering glass.

'Let's go,' she said.

2 Commander Allan Dice woke shortly after 6 a.m. He turned over and tried to get back to sleep but after half an hour he gave up and eased himself gently out from under the bedclothes, careful not to wake his wife.

He stood at the foot of the bed and looked at her, peering in the dim early-morning light. Only her face was showing above the covers.

Her short blonde hair was in disarray, exposing the brown at the roots. She still wore the remains of the previous night's make-up but it did not hide the unnatural whiteness of her face and the dark rings under her eyes. On the far side of the bed her clothing lay scattered on the floor. She was breathing heavily with her mouth open, almost snoring, and beads of sweat glistened dully on her forehead.

Dice went to the bathroom, washed and shaved, then returned to the bedroom and dressed silently. His wife stirred as he left the room but she did not wake.

He made his own breakfast, then sat reading the previous day's newspaper. When the telephone rang he threw down the paper and hurried into the hall to answer, anxious that his wife should not wake. He knew that the call meant trouble. It was a penalty of his profession that a telephone call could never be presumed to be innocent.

The caller was Detective Sergeant Stennet, the Anti-Terrorist Squad night duty officer. Stennet gave a brief and lucid explanation of what had occurred.

'Send a car for me immediately,' Dice ordered.

'It's already on the way, sir,' Stennet said.

Dice returned to the kitchen, picked up his paper and turned to the editorial, blanking his mind off from what was to come.

He had learned over long years to make the best of his rare moments of peace and quiet.

3 CODE SK 15 D. FROM KOSHELEV ZURICH REFERENTURA TO DIAKENOV EXECUTIVE ACTION DEPARTMENT 1ST CHIEF DIRECTORATE.

RELIABLE INFORMATION BREAKAWAY ACTION COMMITTEE INTERNATIONAL WORKERS BROTHERHOOD PLAN INDEPENDENT WET AFFAIR U.K. TARGETS ALEXANDER POPE MP/PAUL CARPENTER REPRESENTATIVES EMERGENT UK CHRISTIAN DEMOCRAT PARTY. AGENTS ALREADY DISPATCHED. ELIAS PINA CHAIRMAN IWB RECALCITRANT. INSTRUCTIONS. END.

4 CODE SK 15 D. FROM DIAKENOV EXECUTIVE ACTION DEPARTMENT 1ST CHIEF DIRECTORATE TO KOSHELEV ZURICH REFERENTURA.

CAPITALIST MARTYRS UNDESIRABLE. CLOSE ZURICH OFFICE IWB. DETAIN PINA AWAIT KGB ESCORT. FURTHER ACTION RESERVED THIS OFFICE ONLY. DESTRUCT NOTICE APPLIES. END.

5 The Reverend Paul Carpenter woke early and, as was his habit, got up immediately. He washed and dressed and prepared himself a light breakfast.

Afterwards he made his bed but left the washing-up in the sink. His secretary, Mary Tü, liked to perform small personal services for him, perpetuating her own myth about him, that he was capable of caring for others but not for himself.

At 7 a.m. he left his first-floor flat in Spencer Road and walked the short distance to Hampstead Heath. Already the morning commuter traffic was building up along Heath Road and he ran the gauntlet of the hurrying cars to cross on to the Heath itself.

A fair was camped alongside Heath Road, on a space which was usually a car park. At this hour there was no sign of movement amongst the stalls and caravans. The encampment looked tawdry and exhausted, hungover from a surfeit of moneymaking, like a drunk caught unawares in early morning sleep.

Carpenter walked as far as the first pond, then turned back, retracing his steps to the flat. He felt faintly resentful at having to cut short his walk. These days it was the only exercise he managed to get, but he had a particularly heavy schedule ahead of him and his pleasures, small though they were, must ever take second place to his work.

Mary Tü had not arrived by the time he returned to the flat and he set about checking his notes for the important meeting arranged with Alexander Pope M.P. for 11 a.m. that morning. The subject was the integration of anti-pollution measures into the ruralization policies already adopted by the Christian Democrat Party of which Pope was the sole parliamentary representative and he, Carpenter, Chairman of the Executive Committee.

During his walk, Carpenter had thought of a slogan to encapsulate the urgency of the measures they proposed. He mulled it over, honed it, and finally added it to his notes.

He wrote: 'Pollution will cost you the Earth.'

After a moment's reflection he added an exclamation mark.

6 Even before the sound of the explosion at New Scotland Yard had died away the car was driving out of Monck Street, heading down Horseferry Road towards the Embankment. It turned into Millbank and a few moments later turned off the main road into the centre of a large block of service flats built round a square courtyard.

The man parked in the courtyard. He and the girl left the car and walked towards an entrance on the far side. He was carrying one of the holdalls.

They ignored the lift and took the stairs up to the fourth floor where they stopped outside a door marked 413B. There was no one in sight, no sound of movement.

The man put the holdall on the ground and took from it two automatic rifles. He checked them quickly, then handed one to the girl.

She pressed the doorbell.

Alexander Pope answered the door. There was no mistaking him. He lived his life these days in a blaze of publicity.

He was dressed in his pyjamas and his eyes were still bleary with sleep. His reactions were predictably slow, but he had half turned to run when the first bullets smashed into his body, throwing him back into the hallway of his flat.

The girl stepped forward and fired a short burst into his head at point-blank range.

A woman wearing only a nightdress appeared at the end of the hallway, stared in disbelief, then began to scream. The girl raised the barrel of her automatic rifle and the scream died as the bullets traced a pattern of holes across the woman's nightdress from her right thigh to her left shoulder.

The man replaced his gun in the holdall and held it open for the girl to do the same.

They ran back down the stairs, then walked calmly across the courtyard to the car.

Behind them doors slammed and a woman screamed.

The man drove carefully out of the courtyard and joined the flow of traffic along Millbank towards Parliament Square.

The girl felt the excitement of the killing riding high in her, but she forced her voice to remain calm.

'Two down, one to go,' she said.

7 Commander Dice arrived at New Scotland Yard at 7.50 a.m. The building had been evacuated and the adjacent roads closed, bringing chaos to the traffic in Victoria Street.

He went straight to the scene of the explosion on the third floor. The damage was bad enough, the toilets were barely identifiable as such, but he had seen much worse. The bomb had obviously been of no great size.

Assistant Commissioner Cottar was standing in the shattered corridor near where the toilets had been, talking to a group of officers which included Chief Superintendent Ray Corelli, Dice's second-in-command on the Anti-Terrorist Squad, and Commander Mike Delabole of C.11, the department devoted to criminal intelligence and what was euphemistically termed 'technical support'.

Not for the first time Dice reflected on how much of a senior officer's time was spent just talking. True, they were the decision-makers, but they worked in a strange vacuum, often divorced from the centre of action, one step removed from the junior officers who had the close contact with events that Dice so missed. To the uninitiated it must seem that it was the junior officers who did the work, the senior officers who collected the credit.

Now there would be more talking. Talking here at the scene, talking on the telephone, talking at the inevitable conferences. The prospect did not please Dice. He was a man of few words.

The Assistant Commissioner turned to see who had arrived. His face was stiff with anger. He had known, as they all had, that sooner or later someone would take a crack at the Yard, but the knowledge did nothing to soften the blow to police pride and prestige.

'A fine kettle of fish, Dice,' said Cottar, frowning at the Commander as if he were responsible.

'Indeed it is, sir,' said Dice neutrally, peering round Cottar's bulk to look into the shattered toilets.

All he could see was the expansive backside of Colonel Tom Watkins, the Home Office Bomb Disposal expert, bent over a pile of rubble. The air in the corridor was still heavy with masonry dust and there was half an inch of water on the floor.

'Bastards!' said Cottar, to no one in particular.

'How far have we got, Ray?' Dice asked.

Chief Superintendent Corelli counted on his fingers, ticking off items one at a time.

'Mr Cottar had already evacuated the building by the time I arrived, it's being searched now on a priority for reoccupation basis. All officers on the call-out list have been informed. I have pulled in our whole squad, including those on leave. Special Patrol Groups are working with "A" Division to seal off the immediate area and we have the usual stop on stations, bus terminals and so on. The trouble is . . .'

'The horse has bolted,' Dice supplied.

'And what's worse, we don't even know what the horse looked like.'

Dice looked across to Commander Delabole.

'Do we have any intelligence, Mike?'

Mike Delabole made a face and gave the thumbs down sign.

'If we'd had the slightest buzz of anything like this, old chap, you'd have known about it.'

Delabole affected a languid, dated manner of speech. He thought it gave him an aura of detached superiority. He was alone in this assessment.

'No ideas?' Dice asked.

In the background Assistant Commissioner Cottar sniffed loudly.

'No. I've spoken to Special Branch, Colin Land is coming over . . . but there again, if he'd known anything . . .'

Dice nodded.

'It was a small one, token really. They'll get what they want, publicity,' Delabole opined.

'And how, sir,' said Corelli wryly. 'We're going to be the laughing stock of the world.'

Assistant Commissioner Cottar blew his nose loudly, then flapped the handkerchief at them.

'Can you imagine how the Commissioner is going to take this, eh?' he asked.

The company accepted the question as rhetorical. Sir John Cowling was a fairly humourless individual at the best of times, and a political animal always. It was certain he would be displeased.

'I gather there were no casualties,' said Dice.

'One cleaner, shock and a couple of cuts, that's all,' Corelli answered.

'Thank God for that,' Dice said.

'Luck!' said Cottar firmly. 'Just pure bloody luck.'

'Do you want any of my men to help you with the security investigation, sir?' Dice asked.

'That is already in hand, thank you Dice,' Cottar said, pulling out his handkerchief again.

He suffered from hay fever. It seemed to get worse when he was under stress. Since, as Assistant Commissioner Crime, he was the senior officer in charge of the physical security of the New Scotland Yard building, he was suffering particularly badly at that moment.

'No signs of a break-in, I suppose?' Dice enquired.

Cottar was getting close to boiling point. He blew loudly, scrubbed at his nose with the handkerchief and stared belligerently at Dice.

'No, Dice. So far as we know there has been no forced entry to the building,' he said heavily. 'Would you like me to list the alternatives?'

'No, sir. Thank you,' said Dice.

'You are welcome,' Cottar said, sniffing loudly.

'If you will excuse me, sir, I think I will be better employed in my office,' said Dice, diplomatically.

'No doubt.'

And Cottar turned his back on Dice to stare pointedly into the remains of the toilet.

Chief Superintendent Corelli worried about his immediate senior. In some ways Dice seemed painfully naïve. Surely he realized that Cottar had his knife into him and that an incident like this would exacerbate rather than relieve the internal politics of the force? Yet Dice went on his own sweet monosyllabic way, apparently indifferent to his future prospects.

Commander Mike Delabole was different again. He could recognize a rung of the advantage ladder at fifty paces in total darkness. As Dice and Corelli left he edged over to stand beside the Assistant Commissioner.

'I've given the matter thought, sir,' he said, 'but I can conceive of nothing further that we can do that you have not already put in hand.'

'Experience,' said Cottar, much mollified, 'just a matter of experience, Mike!'

But they both knew that he was not going to come out of this affair with an enhanced reputation. Delabole was already casting around in his mind for another star to hitch himself to.

Dice was deep in thought as he walked along the corridor with Corelli. He did not speak until they were waiting for the lift.

'This team, they're not any of our regulars,' he said.

'No?'

'I smell strangers.'

'New boys?'

'Perhaps.'

'That's going to make things difficult.'

'Yes.'

'I assume we are taking charge of the investigation?'

'That's for the Commissioner to say.'

'Mr Cottar could have given us the word just now, we could make a start if we knew.'

'We make a start anyway.'

'And you think this is a brand new team?'

'I do.'

'Why?'

'Call it intuition.'

The lift arrived and they got in. As they rose to the floor that housed the Anti-Terrorist Squad Offices, Corelli considered the implications of what Dice had said. It did not occur to him that Dice could be in error.

'D'you think Mr Delabole was right, they were out for publicity?' he asked.

Dice said nothing. He stood staring at the blank wall of the lift, deep in thought. Corelli waited.

'No, not publicity. Well, partly perhaps,' Dice said eventually.

The lift slid silently to a halt and the two men stepped out into the corridor. Immediately opposite them the main office of the Anti-Terrorist Squad was a hive of activity, telephones ringing, officers running, talking at the tops of their voices, typewriters clattering. Dice led the way into the relative quiet of his office and waved Corelli to a chair.

'If not publicity, what then?' Corelli asked. 'If they wanted to kill policemen they picked the wrong time of day, they'd have realized that.'

'What's on the floor immediately above those toilets, Ray?' Dice asked, suddenly.

'The Traffic Department typing pool.'

'Oh.'

'And below it are the Central Traffic Control Offices.'

'And above the typing pool?'

'Information Room.'

Dice stabbed a finger at Corelli's chest.

'Of course! That's it, Ray. *That's* what they were after.'

Corelli shrugged.

'Then they missed it by two floors. If they were good enough to get in with the bomb, then out again undetected, would they have made an elementary mistake like that?'

Dice launched into what was, for him, a mammoth speech.

'There are two possibilities. Either they knew the layout of the Yard but made a mistake by one floor, one floor mark you, not two, because they intended to get underneath the target knowing Information Room would be staffed; or they planted it just anywhere, hoping that I.R. would be evacuated with the rest of the building. And they were right, that was exactly what happened. Either way, they needed to put our eyes and ears out of action for a while. They have another job planned and to pull it off they needed to cut communications between the Yard and Divisions.'

'Could be . . .' said Corelli, doubtfully.

'I.R. will have moved to the emergency layout in the basement, that right?'

'Yes.'

'But Information Room is top of the priority list for re-occupation in the event of an incident, so how long were we totally out of communication?'

'Perhaps four or five minutes, no more.'

'They may have expected longer.'

'But if anything had happened, we'd have heard.'

'It might not be a bomb. Is I.R. back in its own offices?'

'I believe so.'

'Ask them.'

Corelli asked. But the duty Inspector at Information Room had only routine matters to report at that time.

'What do you think, sir?' Corelli asked.

'We wait,' Dice said.

8 Mary Tü walked from Hampstead underground station to the Reverend Paul Carpenter's flat in Spencer Road. She passed two Water Board workmen digging a hole on one side of Willoughby Road. They looked up, grinned and whistled appreciatively.

'Don't fall down the 'ole, luv,' said one.

'Mornin' beautiful,' said the other.

Mary Tü smiled at them and waved.

'God bless you,' she said.

She heard a snatch of their conversation as she walked on.

'D'you reckon it's right, what they say about them Chinese girls? You know, about them bein' sideways on . . .?'

Then she turned into Spencer Road and heard no more. She did not resent the men's vulgarity, nor did it disturb her. Time was when she would have sold her body to either of them and thought nothing of it. Then she had heard Paul Carpenter speak, and Jesus had come into her life.

She had regained her innocence, found a peace of mind beyond her previous experience. She had been forgiven, her whole life had changed and her gratitude to Paul Carpenter was boundless.

He let her into the flat. His greeting was cursory, distracted. She recognized the symptoms, Carpenter was immersed in his work.

She followed him into the living area, at one end of which were two desks. Carpenter sat down at the larger one near the window overlooking the road and returned to a perusal of his notes.

'What would you like me to do first, Paul?' she asked.

He looked up at her and smiled vaguely.

'Oh . . . you could type tomorrow's speech, I've rewritten it, it's on your desk somewhere . . . there's no hurry though.'

Mary returned his smile, nodded briskly and walked across the room to the kitchen area where she found the breakfast dishes in the sink. She much preferred the days when they worked here, at the flat. There were then personal things she could do for him, some small repayment she could make.

She began to wash up the dishes. Paul could perform miracles for others, but he was quite incapable of doing the smallest thing for himself.

9 The terrorists' car was well clear of Parliament Square before the police sealed off the area as a result of the Scotland Yard bomb.

They threaded their way carefully through the now heavy traffic, along Whitehall, round Trafalgar Square and into the Strand.

The man had driven the route several times before at exactly this time of day. He knew every inch of the way, every police traffic point, and he had timed the run to the minute.

He drove up Kingsway and headed north through Holborn,

Euston and on into Camden Town. There he turned off Camden High Street into a maze of side roads and eventually pulled off the road through two broken metal gates on to an open site that had been cleared for rebuilding.

It had been some time since the original buildings had been demolished and the area enclosed with wire fencing, and it had inevitably been vandalized. The broken gates gave unrestricted access and long since the site had become a prime spot for free overnight parking, for the deposit of rubbish and the abandonment of unwanted vehicles.

They parked between the rusting hulk of an old Jaguar saloon and a fairly new 15-cwt van in one corner of the site. Not far from this spot was an old wooden packing case, lying on its side and part filled with a bundle of filthy old rags. The man got out of the car and looked around.

'Okay,' he said.

'You stay out there while I change. Keep your eyes open,' the girl instructed him.

He shrugged. Not long before she had stripped to practically nothing in front of him. Now she was being coy. Who could understand women?

Two minutes later she stepped out of the car wearing a tight sweater, neat skirt and fashionable shoes.

'Move yourself,' she said.

They took two of the holdalls and put them in the back of the 15-cwt van, then got in and drove away in the direction of Hampstead.

A few minutes later, the bundle of rags in the old wooden packing case moved.

Tom Bowling knew a good thing when he saw it. Those two had been up to no good, and they hadn't locked that car, he was sure.

But his expert search of the car revealed nothing but one holdall. He did not empty it, just opened it to check the contents. It was then obvious that it contained only women's clothing. Not much of a haul, but something for nothing.

He closed the holdall and tucked it away in the back of the old packing case amongst his other treasures.

He could tell from the set of the sun that it would be a while yet before Jack Gold opened for business.

10 'They killed Alexander Pope,' said Corelli.

Dice stared at him, stunned into momentary silence.

'The Member of Parliament. Machine pistol, automatic rifle, one of the two. You were right, it seems.'

Corelli took a seat opposite Dice's desk and made a hopeless gesture with his hands.

'Nobody saw anything.'

'What time?' asked Dice.

'About seven-thirty.'

'Where?'

'His London flat, just off Millbank.'

'Vehicle?'

'I suppose so. Nobody saw it.'

'Who's in charge there?'

'Chambers. Shall we go?'

'You go, Ray. I've seen enough dead bodies. Take Inspector Coates with you, leave him there as liaison for us.'

'Right. You'll come down later?'

'No. If there's anything for us, you and Coates will find it. Get back as soon as you can.'

Corelli stood to leave.

'Ray . . .'

'Yes sir?'

'Is Inspector Beal in the office?'

'Yes.'

'On your way out, tell him to check the potential target index, bring in the file on the Christian Democrat Party.'

Corelli left and a few moments later Beal entered with the file and laid it on the desk in front of Dice. Dice waved him to a chair and opened the file.

'If you wanted to destroy the Christian Democrats David, who would you kill?' Dice asked.

Inspector Beal thought for a moment.

'As they did, sir. Alexander Pope. He's leader of the party, he holds the political power . . . but then . . .'

'Yes?'

'He could probably be replaced . . . perhaps on reflection I'd go for Paul Carpenter. He's the brains, the policy-maker . . . I don't know.'

Dice closed the file and pushed it across the desk. Beal leant forward and picked it up.

'If you wanted to be sure?' Dice asked.

Suddenly Beal saw where his senior officer's questions were leading.

'Both, sir. I'd take out both of them.'

'I agree. Send an S.P.G. team to the party office in Bayswater . . . and one to Carpenter's private address. Do it now.'

11 They parked the van in Worsley Road, Hampstead. The girl got out and walked the short distance to Spencer Road.

There were one or two people about but she saw nothing to rouse her suspicions. She passed the front of Carpenter's block. It was a new building, out of place in a road where most of the dwellings were four-storey Victorian houses converted into flats.

She completed her circuit of the target and returned to the van.

'It's okay,' she said.

They took one holdall each and set off for Spencer Road. On the outside of each holdall was strapped a badminton racquet, a potent mute alibi for two smart-looking young people.

The Special Patrol Group van had been in the yard at Hampstead Police Station, only a few streets away on the corner of Rosslyn Hill and Downshire Hill. The crew were taking their refreshment break when the call came in instructing them to cover Paul Carpenter's home.

They took the back streets to avoid the commuter traffic in

Rosslyn Hill and by this chance saw the terrorists close the rear doors of their van and walk away up Worsley Road.

The Sergeant in charge stopped the vehicle at the junction of Denning Road and Worsley Road to drop off two constables to cover the rear of Paul Carpenter's block. The officers saw the two young people ahead of them carrying holdalls adorned with badminton racquets but they fitted the local scene, looked totally innocent.

When the terrorists saw the S.P.G. vehicle stop and the two officers get out, it looked anything but innocent to them. It seemed certain they would be stopped, questioned and searched. That spelt disaster. The man suddenly had a bad attack of the shakes.

'We've had it, the bastards are coming for us.'

It was the girl who took the initiative.

'Shut your face and get a gun out.'

'They're between us and the van, we're cut off,' he said desperately.

'Do as I tell you,' she spat at him.

'There's too many of them, there's more in the van.'

'Give them a burst then run for the flat, we'll hole up.'

'We've . . .'

But she had a machine pistol in her hands, had dropped her holdall and was swinging round to face the police officers.

Her first burst of fire slaughtered the two unsuspecting policemen on the pavement. Her second shattered the windscreen of the S.P.G. van. Then the man was firing, aiming wildly, and the police van shuddered under a hail of bullets.

'Take the holdalls,' the girl shouted, 'I'll cover you.'

He grabbed the holdalls and set off at a staggering run down Spencer Road . . . the girl stepped back behind a solid brick gate-post, giving herself some cover.

There was a slight movement at the rear of the police van and she took quick aim and fired. The movement ceased.

Then he was shouting at her from the entrance to Carpenter's block.

'Okay, run for it, run!'

She emptied her magazine into the police van, then put her head down and ran, jinking and swerving, towards the sound of his voice.

A bullet thwacked into the garden wall beside her. Then he was firing over her head, screaming abuse at the live remnants of the police patrol.

She scrambled up the entrance steps and ducked down in the porch where he was concealed. Already windows were opening down the street and heads appearing, incautiously exposing themselves.

She fumbled in one of the holdalls, fitted a full magazine to her gun, then handed her colleague a hand grenade.

'I'll take the flat. Give the bastards this, then follow me up.'

He took the grenade, pulled the pin, held it at stiffened arm's length.

The girl pushed open the plate-glass entrance doors and ran into the building. The main stairs faced her. A woman was halfway down the stairs. She stopped, staring anxiously at the doorway. When she saw the girl burst in, gun in hand, she collapsed on the stairs in a dead faint.

The girl kicked her aside as she raced up the stairs.

Outside, the other terrorist exposed himself for a second as he stood up to throw the grenade, but the single shot he attracted was way off target.

The grenade bounced on the road ahead of the police van and rolled forward to rest under the front wheels. He saw two police officers dive away from the vehicle for the cover of the gardens but he was too late to fire at them.

The S.P.G. van exploded violently in a sheet of flame. He turned and ran into the building.

When the girl reached the first floor she found Paul Carpenter and Mary Tü standing together on the landing, looking uncertainly about them. She recognized them both instantly. She had done her homework.

They stared dumbly at her as she threatened them with the gun.

'Back in the flat, move!' she said.

Carpenter put up his hand in a placating gesture and was about to speak. The girl selected single shot and fired once into the wall beside the flat door.

'Get in the passage and lie down flat on your faces,' she commanded.

Carpenter and Mary Tü did as they were told. The girl stepped over them and turned to cover the door. Then the hand grenade exploded and seconds later the man appeared, wild-eyed and breathless.

'Take over here,' she commanded. 'If the enemy show their faces tell them the score.'

Leaving him in charge of the hostages she set off on a rapid tour of the flat. There were two doors on the right of the passage, a bathroom and toilet, one on the left, which gave on to the living area, and one at the end of the passage which proved to give access to the only bedroom.

She grabbed the covers from the bed and took them into the living area. It was evident that they could not hold the entire flat, and of all the rooms the living area had the best facilities, overlooked the road outside and, most important of all, held the telephone. She dropped the bedclothes on the floor and quickly crossed the room to the curtained french windows.

A police car had parked behind the still burning S.P.G. van, using it as cover. A policeman was ducked behind the car shouting something into a loud-hailer. There was no sign of any other police activity in the road.

There was a sudden short burst of fire from the passage and she ran across the room to the door. Her partner was standing astride the hostages, his gun pointing determinedly along the passage, commanding the stairs through the open front door.

'We've got hostages, you hear? You come in and we'll kill them,' he screamed.

'Okay, bring them in,' she shouted to him.

He managed to kick Paul Carpenter in the side without taking his eyes off the front door.

'Move yourself, in there . . .'

The hostages got to their feet and were bundled into the front room. The girl slammed the door behind them, then covered them with her gun.

'Get the desks. Against the door,' she ordered.

As the man hauled the desks across the room to block the only door, Carpenter spoke for the first time.

'This is no good you know . . .'

He got no further. The girl stepped forward and hit him in the face with the butt of her gun. Carpenter fell to the floor, blood spilling from his mouth.

Mary Tü started forward in his defence, puny fists upraised. The girl grinned viciously and jabbed the barrel of her rifle forward into her body. Mary collapsed on the floor beside Carpenter, clutching her stomach.

'Take over here,' the girl said when her partner had completed his task. 'I must get on the phone before they tap it.'

The telephone was standing on a cupboard in the kitchen area. She dialled a number. As she listened to the ringing tone she spoke over her shoulder.

'Talk to them. Tell them a story,' she said.

He spoke loudly, drowned the sound of the girl's voice on the telephone.

'Listen Carpenter, and you, chinky, if you want to stay alive you both keep very quiet and do as you're told. One bad move, one wrong sound and you're dead. Understand? We don't care, see, we don't care if you live or die, makes no difference to us.'

The girl had finished speaking. She listened for a few moments, nodding her head as if in agreement. Then she replaced the receiver and ripped the wire from its wall socket.

'It's okay,' she said.

'Fixed?'

'Fixed.'

'When?'

'Don't be stupid. Hang on to them while I look around.'

She conducted a quick but thorough appraisal of the room. It was carpeted wall to wall but the carpet was old and worn. Apart from the two desks, now moved, the far end boasted a settee and two armchairs, the two upright chairs that had served the desks, a standard lamp and two occasional tables. There was a fixed picture window which looked out on to the balcony and the road. The girl pulled the curtains across and moved on.

The kitchen area consisted of a sink and double draining board, cooker, refrigerator and a range of cupboards in front of which stood a cheap dining table with four wooden chairs. In the centre of the table stood a small transistor radio. The french windows were set in the front facing wall opposite the dining table and were curtained to the floor with net and a heavier material. She left the heavy curtains open and peered out from behind them.

The balcony ran the width of the building and was about six feet in depth with a low brick wall to the front and sides, topped by a metal balustrade. There was nothing on the balcony except half a dozen tomato plants growing in plastic bags containing a manufactured growth media. The plants were tied to stakes by stout red twine.

Out in the road things were hotting up. There were now three police cars in evidence and uniformed officers were hurrying people along the pavements, obviously evacuating the area. The girl turned away, there were things yet to be done before the net closed in on them completely.

She began opening cupboards and drawers in the kitchen area. In one she found a ball of red twine and in another some cleaning rags. She carried them across to where her partner still menaced the hostages and threw the items on the floor.

'Tie them up, gag them,' she said.

Whilst he was engaged in this task she collected every container she could find that would hold water and filled them at the kitchen sink. She knew well that at the first opportunity the police would cut off all services to the flat. It was part of the tactics, part of the game.

Food presented a bigger problem. Her search revealed one loaf of bread, a dozen eggs, some margarine, six carrots, an onion, a packet of frozen peas, seven potatoes, some instant coffee and a tin of pork luncheon meat. It was not enough. Toilet facilities were of course non-existent. Still, they had cards to play, with any luck the police could be persuaded to supply what they needed to last out.

She saw no reason why their stay should be more unpleasant than was necessary.

The man left the hostages on the floor side by side, their legs tied together at the ankles, wrists bound behind their backs, the gags rammed into their mouths and held in place by twine tied behind their heads.

Carpenter had his eyes closed and blood from his battered mouth was seeping through the gag. The girl was retching silently, her body contorting, her face pressed against the floor.

'They're in the hall, I heard them,' he said.

The girl crossed the room and listened at the door. She heard scufflings and muted voices.

'We'd better convince them we mean business,' she said.

'You think they don't know?'

'When I fire, put one through the door.'

She crossed to the french windows, setting the automatic rifle to single shot. There were a number of targets available. She selected a police inspector who was standing beside a patrol car, leaning in the passenger side, talking on the car radio.

Her shot shattered the windscreen of the police car and sent the inspector tumbling for cover.

Her partner fired through the door.

'Piss off you bastards, you want them to die?' he yelled.

The girl laughed, suddenly, almost hysterically.

He spun round at her, angry, thinking that she was laughing at him.

'What's so bloody funny?'

'I missed. No more than fifty yards, and I missed the bastard!'

12 Sir John Cowling chaired the meeting he had called in the sixth-floor senior officers' conference room at New Scotland Yard.

He looked grim. He sat immaculate and motionless, his eyes fixed unswervingly on each speaker in turn as his senior officers reported the status of their responsibilities.

Assistant Commissioner Cottar began. He reiterated the mechanics of the physical defence of the Yard building.

Sir John cut him short, brought him to the present.

Cottar was perspiring freely despite the air conditioning, and his hay fever was troubling him persistently.

He ran through the timetable of events, the actions he had taken.

'Conclusions?' the Commissioner asked, abruptly.

'Entrance and exit were gained through one of the staffed entrances, by deception.'

'Thank you Roy.'

To Cottar it sounded as if the Commissioner was pronouncing the death sentence. He sneezed loudly and disappeared into his handkerchief.

Sir John's eyes passed on to rest on Commander Allan Dice.

'Mr Corelli will report the circumstances of the murder of Mr and Mrs Pope, sir,' Dice said.

Their eyes flickered to rest on Corelli.

Corelli made his report.

'Suspects?' asked the Commissioner.

'No, sir. None,' said Corelli.

'Forensic information?'

'Not yet, sir.'

'Colin?' said Sir John.

Commander Colin Land, Special Branch, made a neat and brief speech outlining the possible motives of the attackers, but he was of necessity vague.

'You have nothing for us then,' the Commissioner stated bluntly.

'Not as yet, sir, I'm pulling out all stops.'

The Commissioner's eyes passed on.

'Mike?'

Commander Delabole was also pulling out all stops, but had nothing to contribute. Nor had Deputy Assistant Commissioner (Operations) Ben Yallop, nor had any of the four senior uniformed officers present.

'Comments?' asked the Commissioner of the assembled company.

Dice cleared his throat and raised a tentative finger.

'Yes, Allan?'

Only the Commissioner ever addressed Dice by his Christian name. His other colleagues, his few friends, his wife, all called him simply Dice. Even his junior officers, calling him 'Sir' to his face, called him Dice behind his back. The name fitted him as Allan did not. Only the Commissioner ever called him Allan.

'I think the two cases are related,' said Dice.

In the background Assistant Commissioner Cottar harrumphed loudly.

'Why?' asked Sir John.

Dice explained.

'I refer you to paragraph seven, section two of the Serious Incident Instructions of this year, relating to command structure in the event of multiple related incidents,' he ended.

'Comments?' asked Sir John, opening the debate to the room.

'Unproven,' said Cottar, sniffing. 'We have two separate enquiries here.'

The Commissioner turned back to Dice but it was Deputy Assistant Commissioner Yallop who spoke.

'I think Dice is quite right, sir. His theory makes sense.'

Cottar glared across the table at his old enemy. He should have expected Yallop to support Dice, pour salt in the wounds.

'On the face of it the incident here is a matter for the Anti-Terrorist Squad; the Pope killings seem to come under the jurisdiction of the Serious Crimes Squad,' said the Commissioner.

Cottar hid a triumphant smile behind his handkerchief.

'On the face of it, yes, sir,' said Yallop. 'However, such facts as we have suggest a definite possibility of a relationship between the two incidents. I submit we cannot chance a divided enquiry.'

Yallop looked thoughtfully at the back of his hand. Cottar looked expectantly at the Commissioner. Dice sat back in his chair and waited for the decision.

The telephone in front of the Commissioner shattered the moment. It had to be urgent, no one would lightly interrupt such a high-powered meeting.

The Commissioner answered, listened, then said: 'Send him in.'

Detective Inspector David Beal entered the room and stood uncertainly just inside the door. All eyes in the room were on him.

'Yes, Mr Beal. Tell us what happened,' the Commissioner said.

Dice was on the edge of his seat, watching his officer closely.

'Acting on the instructions of Commander Dice, I sent an S.P.G. patrol to the home address of Mr Paul Carpenter, sir,' Beal began.

'Where?' asked the Commissioner.

'Spencer Road, Hampstead, sir.'

'Yes. Go on.'

'We don't know the details yet, sir. When they arrived in the street outside, a man and a woman opened fire on them, a sergeant and two P.C.s are dead. The assailants ran into a flat, they've taken hostages.'

'Whose flat is it?' Dice cut in.

'The Reverend Paul Carpenter's, sir.'

'Anything else?' asked the Commissioner.

'No, sir.'

'Who are the hostages?'

'We assume the Reverend Carpenter and possibly his

secretary, a girl named Mary Tü, sir.'

'Thank you, Mr Beal.'

Beal acknowledged his dismissal and left the room.

The silence was charged with anger. There could be no rejoicing at the cornering of the killers when five people were already dead.

'Then we have a siege situation,' said the Commissioner.

Dice stood up.

'With your permission, sir.'

The Commissioner nodded.

'Assume executive command,' he said. 'The three incidents will be investigated by the Anti-Terrorist Squad, as one. This matter has political connotations, you will confer with me on all matters of policy.'

Dice left the room, followed by Corelli. Cottar blew his nose loudly. It was not one of his better days.

The Commissioner got to his feet, leaned forward on the long, polished table, balancing on his knuckles.

'Gentlemen,' he said, 'we all have work to do.'

He returned to his office and buzzed for his secretary.

'Get me the Home Secretary,' he said.

As he waited he made notes, preparing what he would say. He was acutely conscious of the necessity of choosing the right words, the right phraseology.

He selected his tone of voice, sincere regret tinged with guarded optimism. He thought he could afford that.

His telephone rang.

13 By the time Dice and Corelli arrived at Spencer Road the area had been cordoned off and the nearby houses evacuated. Their car dropped them at the police barrier at the end of the road. The whole area was alive with policemen and police vehicles.

They sought out the young Detective Chief Inspector who had taken early charge of the situation.

'Chief Inspector Kent, sir,' he said.

'Are we in the flat, Mr Kent?' Dice asked.

'Yes, sir. They have the hostages in one room, at the front. We hold the rest of the flat.'

'How many officers have we?'

'Just the S.P.G. officers and a dozen P.C.s. I've placed them in the flat. Reinforcements are on the way.'

'How long have you been here?'

'About ten minutes, sir.'

'Have we established any kind of contact?'

'No, sir. They're still sniping at us. A short while ago they shot at an inspector and they've fired through the flat door into the hall once.'

'Anyone hurt?'

'No, sir.'

'Can you get me into the flat?'

'Yes, sir.'

Dice turned to Corelli.

'I'm going in. You might as well get things moving, Ray.'

Corelli nodded. It was his responsibility to see to the administration of the incident: the staffing and staff rotas; the provision of a control post and communications, office equipment, canteen and toilet facilities; the provision and supervision of armaments and technical support services; liaison between Dice and the other police departments involved; representatives of non-police advisers such as the local council, the army and the medical services.

Corelli had plenty to do.

Dice followed the young Chief Inspector to the barrier at the end of Spencer Road. The officer pointed ahead.

'The new building on the right, sir. Middle flat.'

Dice stared. There was no sign of movement in the flat. He noted the balcony in front of the window, measured with his eye the distance between that and the one above. He nodded to the Chief Inspector.

'Right. Let's go in.'

'This way, sir.'

Kent led him down a side road, through a gate into the rear garden of the end house in Spencer Road. A stepladder was set against the far wall. They climbed six garden walls by means of a variety of ladders, dustbins and commandeered chairs, then stood in the rear garden of the new building, now the focal point of the siege. A uniformed officer came to attention, saluted, held the door open for them.

They passed through the ground-floor flat, out into the communal hall, up the stairs to the first floor.

The door of flat B was open, guarded by an armed S.P.G. sergeant, kneeling in the passageway, gun pointing into the flat. He acknowledged his senior officers with a nod, caution taking precedence over protocol.

Dice knelt beside him.

'Have we heard anything?' he asked.

The sergeant shook his head.

'They've barricaded themselves in, sir.' He pointed to the door on the left of the passage. 'We can't get near, if they hear movement they fire through the door.'

Dice nodded, stood up, took off his shoes and walked into the passage. He looked into the bathroom, the toilet and the single bedroom. There were armed S.P.G. officers in each.

Dice moved silently to stand beside the door to the front room. There was a bullet hole at chest height. He put his ear to the door and listened. He heard two voices, male and female, but they were speaking quietly, whispering, and he could not hear what was being said.

He walked carefully down the passage to the front door and put on his shoes.

'What is that room?' he asked Kent.

'Lounge, dining room and kitchen, all in one. I believe Carpenter uses it as an office as well,' the Chief Inspector replied.

'So they have water, cooking facilities, food, heating . . . telephone?'

'Yes, sir.'

'You have the number?'
'Yes, sir.'
'Have you tried ringing it?'
'No, sir. I thought . . .'
'Quite right. There are two hostages?'
'Yes, sir. Carpenter and his secretary, a girl named Mary Tü.'
'Chinese?'
'Half English, half Chinese, born in London.'
'Where did we get our information from?'
'The old lady in the downstairs flat. The terrorists knocked her flying as they came in, she can give a vague description of them, that's all. Bit of a busybody, notes all the comings and goings. She saw Carpenter return from his morning walk, then his secretary arrived. She was just going out when the balloon went up.'
'Carpenter lives here alone?'
'Yes.'
Dice thought for a moment.
'Can we get on to the roof?' he asked.
'Yes, sir.'
'Lead the way.'
Chief Inspector Kent led him up the stairs, past the door of flat C, to a service door at the end of the passage. Behind this a short flight of wooden steps led up to a trapdoor in the roof. It was open. Dice followed Kent up the steps on to the roof.
The roof was flat. A low brick parapet edged it. It offered a partial view across to Hampstead Heath, but this new building was not as tall as the Victorian houses that surrounded it.
At the front of the roof a uniformed S.P.G. officer crouched, holding an issue revolver.
Dice walked across and looked over the front edge, down to the street. The balcony of the top flat obscured his view of the balcony of the flat under siege. Another armed officer crouched on the top balcony, looking down.
Across the road, slightly to his right, the top windows of one of the houses were blanked out with whitewash.

Dice walked back to the trapdoor where Chief Inspector Kent waited.

'I've seen enough,' he said.

When Dice returned to the police barrier at the end of Spencer Road he found Corelli standing in front of a mobile command van, talking to a group of officers, issuing instructions. A post office worker was busily employed at the top of a nearby telegraph pole, linking the command van into the public telephone network.

Dice waited until Corelli joined him. Then he pointed at the command van.

'Quick work.'

'Inspector Beal anticipated some of our needs.'

'Good lad, that,' said Dice.

'Yes, sir.'

'There are some things I want you to find out for me, Ray.'

'Yes, sir. Shall we go in the office?'

'How long will he be?' Dice asked, pointing at the post office employee at the top of the telegraph pole.

'I'll have him tell us the minute we have a line.'

Corelli called an officer across and gave him instructions.

Dice led the way into the command van. It was empty as yet. They sat at a desk and Corelli collected pen and paper to make notes.

'As far as we know there are only two hostages,' Dice said, 'Paul Carpenter and his secretary, Mary Tü. I want a report on the physical and mental health of both of them from their own doctors.'

Corelli wrote rapidly.

'I want all the officers on duty within the operational area to be armed. They outgun us at the moment.'

'That's already in hand, sir,' said Corelli.

'There's a house on the opposite side of Spencer Road from the flat, the top floor is empty. Get permission from the owners for us to use it.'

'Instead of the command van?' Corelli asked.

'No. As well as. We'll keep the monitoring equipment up there. I want to be near them, where I can see them.'

Corelli scribbled.

'Put a couple of beds up there, Ray, we might need them.'

'Anything else, sir?'

'Yes. Find out how much food there is in the flat.'

Corelli hesitated.

'There's an old lady from flat A, she knows everything that goes on in the building, maybe she saw Carpenter or the girl come back from shopping. Ask her.'

'I'll try, sir.'

'The flat is all electric. Have the Electricity Board cut the supply, same for the water, soon as possible.'

'I've spoken to the regional superintendents of both, sir. They're just waiting for the word.'

There was a brief knock on the door and a face appeared.

'You have a line now, sir,' said the officer.

Dice took a crumpled piece of paper from his pocket. On it he had written the telephone number of the flat, as supplied by Chief Inspector Kent.

He pulled the telephone across the desk towards him and dialled the number.

He got the unobtainable signal.

Dice dialled twice more with exactly the same result. He replaced the receiver and looked at Corelli.

'They've ripped out the phone,' he said.

Corelli scratched his ear and stared into space.

'So. They don't want to talk to us.'

Dice looked at his watch. It was 10 a.m.

'Not yet,' he said.

14 Tom Bowler, gentleman of the road, had no friends and few acquaintances. Yet he was a well-known figure in the streets of Camden Town. Even people who did not know him personally, had never spoken to him, would never wish to, knew that his nickname was 'Smiler'. This for the perverse reason that he was of permanently lugubrious demeanour.

Smiler made his way to the shop owned by Jack Gold, one of his few acquaintances. Under his arm he had the holdall of clothes that he had stolen from the small saloon car with the tinted windows.

In the front window of Jack Gold's shop hung a row of second-hand suits. The remaining space was cluttered with a quite incredible array of chipped, rusted and broken bric-à-brac. The sign painted in faded, peeling letters above the shop window declared that Jack Gold was a dealer in high-class antiques.

Smiler went round the back of the shop, let himself into the rear yard, knocked on a door and waited.

Jack Gold recognized his visitor, noted the holdall under his arm, and somewhat reluctantly, for the smell of the man offended him, let Smiler into the small back room and closed the door against prying eyes.

'What you got, Smiler?' he asked.

'Clothes,' said Smiler, 'good stuff.'

He placed the holdall on an elderly trestle table and, with an expansive gesture, invited Jack Gold to open it.

'Good stuff. Quality stuff.'

The dealer opened the holdall, took out the clothes one piece at a time, inspected them disdainfully and dropped them on the table.

The fourth item he pulled out was a woman police officer's uniform jacket. He stared at it in horror, holding it at arm's length between finger and thumb, as if it were infected.

Smiler began to edge towards the door.

'Mr Gold . . . I swear . . .'

Jack Gold did not look athletic. But the hand dropped the offending jacket and Gold covered the distance between them before Smiler had time to turn and run.

'You stinking squealer!' he raged, grasping Smiler by the hair.

'No, no, Mr Gold, I swear! . . .'

'You were tryin' to set me up, weren't you?'

'No . . .'

But Gold knew what he knew. He trusted his eyes, his ears, precious little else. He dragged the protesting Smiler through to the shop, held him while he telephoned the police. He hardly noticed the smell now. Anger had dulled his olfactory senses.

No one was going to set up Jack Gold.

15 Dice stood in the hallway of the siege flat. He held a megaphone loosely in his right hand. The officers occupying the flat were still in position but prone on the floor, guns trained on the door to the front room.

It was silent, but there was an aura of excitement, of nervous expectancy.

Dice moved across to stand beside the door to the front room, his back against the passage wall. He raised the megaphone to his lips and aimed it at the door.

'This is Commander Dice. The building is surrounded by armed police. I ask you to send out the hostages, then put down your arms and surrender yourselves. Your position is hopeless.'

Dice waited. There was no sound from the room. He raised the megaphone again.

'If you surrender peaceably and do no harm to the hostages I can assure you of fair treatment, a fair trial.'

Again he waited. There was a shuffling movement in the room but no reply.

'Your position is hopeless. It is only a matter of time . . .'

The sharp crack of the automatic rifle was instantaneous with the bullet smashing through the door and embedding itself in the far wall with a dull thud.

Dice stood absolutely still for a moment, then walked to the front door of the flat and handed the megaphone to Chief Inspector Kent.

'Try them once an hour. Keep your head down, you know what to expect.'

'Yes, sir.'

'Let me know what reaction you get.'

Dice went up to the top flat, entered and found his way to the balcony where officers were erecting a block and tackle intended for the transfer of food and other items to the flat below should the siege progress in that direction. They acknowledged him with a glance or a nod but continued with their work.

He could see that it would have been possible to enclose the balcony below completely with wooden screens, denying the terrorists light and a view of the street, eradicating the field of fire from the balcony, enabling police to move about freely in Spencer Road, and having the psychological effect of making the terrorists feel enclosed, trapped. But Dice abandoned the idea, attractive as it was. The situation was too volatile, such a provocative act could easily unleash a violent reaction.

Dice made his way back to the mobile command van at the end of Spencer Road. Here wooden shutters ten feet high already blocked off the command van from a sight of the siege flat and officers were busily engaged in continuing the erection of a similar barrier along both sides of Spencer Road itself. Soon the police would be able to move freely up and down the road, and Dice would have ready access to the empty flat he wanted as an advanced command post. He nodded in satisfaction and entered the command van.

The mobile office was now a hive of activity, seemingly overfull with officers talking, typing, telephoning, writing, coming and going. Over this scene of efficient chaos Corelli hovered like a broody hen. He broke off when Dice entered.

'It's coming along, sir,' he said.

'Do we have a plan of the building yet?' Dice asked.

'On the way, sir.'

'I meant the inside of the flat.'

'That's right.'

'Find someone who's been in the flat recently. I want to know exactly what furniture there is, where it is, have it marked on the plan.'

'Right, sir.'

Dice thought for a moment.

'I know they've got automatic rifles, what other weapons have they, do we know?'

'No, sir. They took two large holdalls into the flat with them.'

'They might have more explosives.'

'Could be.'

'Do we have rifles?'

'Yes, sir.'

'How many?'

'Twelve, sir. Nine covering the front, three at the back.'

'Very well. Have the others arrived yet?'

'Mr Delabole and Mr Land are waiting for you in your car. It's about the only place you'll get any peace and quiet at the moment. The Commissioner is coming here in about an hour with Mr Yallop and Mr Cottar. Apparently there's a press conference arranged.'

'There would be,' said Dice.

'Mr Peach is here actually, but he's supervising the fingerprint examination of the terrorists' van. He said he'll speak to you when he's got something to say.'

Dice smiled momentarily. Peach was a man after his own heart.

'By the way, sir, the water and electricity have been cut off to the flat.'

Dice nodded.

'Very well, Ray. You know where I'll be.'

Commanders Land and Delabole were sitting in the back of his car. Dice sat in the front passenger seat, turned to face them, leaning back against the door.

'How goes it, Dice?' Land asked.

'We have them bottled,' said Dice.

'Then be happy, old chap,' said Delabole.

'I smell trouble.'

'Like what?' from Land.

Dice shrugged, pursed his lips.

'I don't know. I don't think they're any of our usual customers.'

'Who then?' Land.

'Maybe *you'll* tell *me*, later.'

'Maybe.'

Dice turned his attention to Commander Delabole.

'I want some gadgets, Mike.'

'You have but to ask.'

'They've pulled out the phone, so we can't tap it. We'll need a landline sooner or later.'

'No problem.'

'Did Ray tell you I intend to use a top flat opposite as a forward command post?'

'He did.'

'I want a wired link microphone in the siege flat, you can get it right up against the door. They even kindly punched a couple of holes through for us.'

'Very decent of them.'

'Could we have a parabolic microphone in the control flat across the road?'

'Not really,' said Delabole, 'you'd be barely in range, twenty-five yards is about top weight for those babies you know, and you'd get awful interference problems. No point, actually. If we can set up a good old-fashioned stethoscope-type microphone, who needs anything else?'

'I was thinking of a back-up, in case they started pumping bullets through the door again.'

'Let them. If they do we can stick it on the dividing wall, just as good.'

'What about reception?'

'A.1. I promise.'

'Very well. Can you set me up a telescope in the control flat, with a light intensifier and image stabilizer? . . . and a stills camera of course . . .'

'Child's play.'

'Now, what about getting a television camera into the flat?'

'You have in mind the flexible eye camera?'

'Yes.'

'I have two at the moment. The longest run between camera and lens in the plasto/metal flex is twenty feet. Is that enough?'

'I should think so. The camera can sit on the top balcony and we can run the flexible eye down the wall.'

'Then where?'

'There's an extractor grille set in the wall at the kitchen end of the room they're in.'

'Fine. But you have the problem of getting it in place without getting your men shot to pieces.'

'I'm aware of that. I shall want all the monitors in the control flat, and tape recorders of course.'

'Your every word is my command,' said Delabole lightly.

'How soon can you start?' asked Dice.

'I have a van-load of goodies parked down the road and men panting to begin. When can you give us safe access?'

'See Ray Corelli. You could start in the flat now, I should think.'

Delabole got out of the car and waved negligently to them. 'Be good,' he said

'I can't help you much at the moment, Dice,' Land said when Delabole had gone.

'I need to know who they are, exactly what their motivation is, not the gumph you gave us at the meeting, Colin.'

'I know. But I need information from you before I can identify them. A name, fingerprints, a look at their weapons, a tape of them talking . . . something.'

'Tomorrow, perhaps tonight.'

A car drew up behind them. Land looked out of the rear window.

'It's God. I think I'll disappear.'

Dice got out of the car and went to meet the Commissioner.

'How are things, Allan?' asked Sir John.

Dice told him.

'A long one, you think?'

'Could be, sir. They have some food, water, they've taken blankets from the bedroom.'

'No toilet facilities though.'

'There's a sink.'

'Mmm. I've spoken to the Home Secretary. We have his permission to call in the Army, the S.A.S.'

'We have plenty of cover, sir.'

'Nevertheless, it shows determination, don't you think? Lets the public see we mean business, intend to stand firm. It might put the fear of God into those blighters in there as well, they have a healthy respect for the S.A.S., and rightly so.'

'When will they be here, sir?'

'An hour or so.'

'I'll tell Corelli.'

'One other thing, Allan. Do they have a battery radio in the flat?'

'We don't know yet, sir. It seems likely.'

'Yes. I'll tell the media we've called in the S.A.S., give the hostages a fillip, let the blighters in there know as well. What about medical support, doctor, psychiatrist?'

'Tomorrow, sir. They'd be wasting their time until we can effectively monitor the flat.'

'I'll leave that titbit for tomorrow's press conference then. Anything else I can impart to the fourth estate?'

'No, sir. I don't think so. It's too early.'

The Commissioner looked at his watch.

'Mustn't keep the gentlemen of the press waiting,' he said.

'No, sir,' said Dice.

16 The man inspected the bound and gagged hostages. Their eyes were open and they were breathing normally.

'They're alive,' he said.

The girl was kneeling on the floor by the french windows, gun in hand, peering upwards for a sight of the officers who had been working at some unknown task on the balcony above.

'Clever bastards. Didn't get a sight of them,' she said.

The man tried the light switch by the door, flicking it several times.

'They've cut off the electricity.'

The girl went to the kitchen sink, turned on the taps. They ran normally.

The man laughed.

'Left us the water then.'

'I doubt it. We've got what's in the tank, that's all,' the girl said.

'It'll be enough.'

'I reckon.'

There was nothing for them to do now. It was a matter of adjusting themselves to the long wait. That would not be easy. The killing, the violent action, the need for instant decisions had brought them to a pitch of tension. The adrenalin still pumped round their bodies, and they moved constantly, prowling round the room, looking out of the windows, fingering their rifles.

The loudhailer started up again.

'This is the police. You are surrounded by armed men. Return the hostages unharmed and you can be sure of a fair trial . . .'

The same old drivel. The man aimed at the door.

'Shall I give them an answer?'

'Waste of time,' the girl said.

She watched him standing there, aimed at the door like a well-trained pointer. Her eyes took in the broad shoulders, the slim hips, the small, rounded buttocks.

'Come here a moment,' she said.

He crossed to her. She moved in close to him, caressed his buttocks with her free hand, whispered in his ear.

'I need it,' she said.

'Now?'

The bluntness of her approach unmanned him for the moment, threw him off balance.

Her hand moved round, touching him, gently at first, then harder. She felt him rise.

'Hell, yes. Right now.'

He looked over his shoulder at the hostages.

'Let them watch. What can they do?' the girl said.

She moved away from him, put her gun on the floor beside the settee that backed against the front wall between the windows, sat down and pulled up her skirt.

'Come on . . .'

He hesitated, wanting but unsure.

The girl pulled down her tights and pants in one movement, lay back on the settee, pulled up her jumper to expose her breasts.

'Come on . . .'

'Suppose they rushed us?'

She was moving her thighs in anticipation, exciting herself with her fingers.

'Hell! They're bloody well not going to, are they?'

'I suppose not.'

He put his gun down beside hers. She watched him as he pulled off his jeans and underpants, revealing his readiness.

Then he was on top of her, into her, and they grasped each other fiercely, expending tension and lust in a fury of sexuality.

Had the police walked in at that moment they would have met with no opposition.

17 Firth left his office in Mayfair at 3 p.m. and walked to Grosvenor Square before he was able to secure a taxi.

The taxi took him to Old Compton Street, Soho. There he paid the driver and watched whilst he drove away. Firth was by nature and training a cautious man.

In the next ten minutes he walked in a circle round Soho, engaging in a number of simple but effective exercises to ensure that he was not under surveillance. Satisfied, he returned to Old Compton Street and stood looking at the photographs on display outside a strip club.

'24-Hour Non-Stop-Strip' said a notice. 'Big Girls Reveal All' said another. 'Our Promise – You see it ALL' said yet another. The photographs on display had white tape stuck modestly across them at an angle, ensuring the customer did not see all without first paying.

Firth paid. The man in the cubicle took his money and gave him a ticket.

'Great show, sir,' he promised.

Firth nodded and went through the door marked 'Entrance'.

Maztikyan watched Firth enter, then sat in the window of the coffee bar opposite the club for another ten minutes before paying his bill. Then he crossed the road and entered the club.

'Great show, sir,' the man promised as Maztikyan paid.

The Russian found Firth in the second row from the back and took a seat beside him. The room was barely lit, small and dingy. It smelt of damp and stale sweat. There were only two other customers and they were in the front row.

On the narrow curtained stage a woman with large breasts was dancing slowly and incompetently to taped music. She wore only a plastic smile and a tired-looking snake.

'You have depraved tastes,' Maztikyan said.

Firth did not take his eyes from the woman.

'I thought it would make a change from the cocktail circuit. Do you think that snake is alive?'

'Plastic, isn't it?'

The stripper went into her final routine. It featured the snake, and probably contravened the laws of obscenity.

'I think it must be,' said Firth as the woman left the stage to the enthusiastic applause of the two men in the front row.

There was no compère. The next girl came on wearing a black leather bikini and an imitation leopard-skin cloak and carrying a candelabra with five black candles. She was short and slim, and she had once been quite pretty.

'They bombed the Yard today,' Firth said conversationally.

'I heard.'

'And assassinated Alexander Pope.'

'Yes. It caused something of a disturbance in the office.'

'I would like to know whose show it was.'

'Not us.'

'You are sure?'

The girl had removed the bikini but still wore the cloak. She was pretending to be reluctant.

'The news caused genuine consternation.'

'I thought it might be the Diakenov's boys.'

'No. I'd have known.'

'They might have chosen not to tell you.'

'I might not have known the details but if this had been a K.G.B. wet affair I'd have known.'

'How?'

'You must take my word for it.'

'Certain things point in that direction.'

'I know. That's what caused the consternation in the office.'

'The matter is urgent, Leonid.'

'But you have them trapped, have you not?'

'Yes. But this affair is political dynamite here. I am under pressure from my masters. They wish to offer guidance to our excellent but unimaginative police force as to the manner in which they should proceed.'

The girl had removed the cloak. The harsh light on the stage revealed the stretch marks on her stomach.

'As of this moment I cannot help you,' Maztikyan said. 'If I hear anything at all that could be relevant I will make contact.'

'Thank you, Leonid. It is urgent.'

'I understand that, Roger.'

Maztikyan left.

Firth stayed. He wanted to see what the girl would do with the black candles.

18 The ten-foot-high wall of linked wooden shutters now joined the barricades at each end of Spencer Road.

Dice and Corelli stood at an observation hole opposite the siege flat, peering anxiously upwards.

On the top balcony stood Mike Delabole and three brawny

uniformed officers. A slim, wiry figure dressed in a track suit and canvas shoes stood precariously on the balcony rail. Between his feet was a pulley wheel over which ran a stout rope attached to a body harness.

They saw Mike Delabole check the body harness, tighten it up against the volunteer's body, then tuck inside it the long flexible metal tube that carried the lens, the eye of the television camera.

Dice had his eyes closed. He crossed himself, then looked up again.

The boy standing exposed on the balcony rail looked frail, vulnerable.

'I'd rather it were me,' said Corelli.

'He's fit, he's young. His chances are better,' said Dice.

'I know. It doesn't make it any easier though, does it?'

'No.'

'I met his wife once. They've got three young children.'

'He will be all right.'

The three uniformed officers were taking up the strain on the rope. The young officer was leaning out from the balcony at an acute angle, testing himself and the rope.

'I hope they oiled that pulley,' said Corelli.

'They did. And he has a bullet-proof waistcoat.'

'Marvellous!' said Corelli bitterly. 'So now they only shoot him in the head or stomach. The slightest sound, that's all. One mistake and the kid's dead.'

'Sometimes it helps to state the obvious, Ray, but not now.'

Corelli stood back from the observation hole, looked at his senior officer.

'I don't have your clinical detachment, Dice. What happens to that boy *matters* to me.'

Dice looked at him, chose to ignore the unusual familiarity, knowing it was bred of respect and anger.

'It matters to me as well,' he said.

'Well then. Do you think they pay that boy enough to go down that rope, risk his life?'

'It isn't a matter of money, Ray. It has to be done. He has to go, we have to watch.'

'Why? Tell me why. Twenty-five years and still I don't know the answer.'

'It's the price we pay for our small freedoms.'

'Politics!'

'A passion for ordering the lives of others is a disease endemic in the human race.'

'Someone should operate,' said Corelli vehemently, 'find an antidote, whatever.'

'Someone did. Pope and Carpenter. That's why that boy is about to risk his life, why Pope is dead, why they will kill Carpenter if we cannot stop them.'

'You think they will?'

'It's what they came for. Whoever they are, they've not come to kill men, they've come to kill an idea.'

'But it won't work. They'll only create martyrs.'

'They've taken that risk. They don't understand they cannot win.'

Dice turned back to the observation hole. Corelli stared at his still, firm profile for a moment, then followed suit.

The boy was perched on the balcony rail, ready to go. Delabole raised his thumb in the direction of the flat. Then, muffled and unintelligible, Dice and Corelli heard Chief Inspector Kent speaking on the loudhailer, providing the boy with the only distraction they could reasonably introduce.

The three officers took the strain as the track-suited figure went over the side, holding himself away from the balcony with his hands. Then he was hanging free, like a spider on a single thread, turning slightly, entirely vulnerable.

Corelli felt the tension. He took a quick look, saw that Dice was gripping the observation hole with both hands, knuckles showing white. There was silence but for the distant metallic voice of the loudhailer.

The boy had both feet on the balcony of the siege flat. He was steadying himself against the wall with one hand. He was perhaps three feet from the grille that covered the vent in the kitchen wall. With his free hand he took the metal flex from beneath the webbing of his body harness, juggled with it until he held it a foot from the eye, then inched along the balcony rail, hand outstretched towards the grille.

'Please God!' whispered Corelli fiercely.

'He will be all right,' Dice repeated, not taking his eyes from the scene.

Commander Delabole was leaning way out over the upper balcony, another officer holding his legs.

The boy had the eyc of the flex inserted in the grille. He took away his hand, slowly, took a step back along the balcony rail, looked up at Delabole, showed him an empty hand.

Then the flex fell from the grille, scraping over the balcony rail, hanging loose from the balcony above, swaying tantalizingly just out of the boy's reach.

'Hell!' Corelli exploded, 'he forgot to use the tape!'

'No. He was trying to make sure he had the angle right. He wants us to have a good picture, see as much as we can before he tapes it in position,' said Dice.

'It *must* have made a noise.'

'If they'd heard, he'd be dead by now,' Dice said.

The boy was swinging loose again, reaching for the flex, tantalizing inches from it. He began a slow swing, limited by the necessity of avoiding sudden contact with the balcony. Then he had the flex in his hand, was reaching for the balcony with his feet, a steadying hand against the wall.

'He *must* hurry,' said Corelli. 'If Kent keeps talking on the loudhailer much longer they'll twig.'

Dice said nothing.

The boy had the flex in his hand, was pushing it in through the grille, twisting it sideways. He took a step back along the rail, watching the grille as if defying the flex to fall again. He showed an empty hand upwards to Delabole.

Commander Delabole squirmed backwards off the upper balcony, disappeared into the upper flat. Seconds later he reappeared, leant over the rail and gave the thumbs-up sign.

The boy edged back to the wall, pulled a strip of black adhesive tape and spent what seemed to the watchers like hours taping the flex firmly in position. Then he was showing his empty hand to Delabole, he was pushing himself free of the balcony, was once more suspended, being inched upwards painfully slowly.

'He's there!' said Corelli. 'He's bloody well made it!'

And the boy was being hauled over the rail of the upper balcony and he was safe.

Dice stood back from the observation hole. His hands were clasped in front of him and his eyes were closed. Sweat stood out on his brow.

'He should get a million-pound bonus for that,' said Corelli.

Dice opened his eyes and looked at Corelli. A smile came and went.

'He'll get the Police Medal. I'll see he does,' Dice said.

19 The command flat consisted of four rooms and the usual offices. Two of these rooms overlooked the road and the siege flat. One of these became the control and monitoring centre, the other, a bedroom, Dice took for his own use.

The flat was completely empty before the police took over, bare boards and empty light sockets. The front windows had been whitewashed over on the inside but Corelli had this cleaned off and replaced with both net and heavy curtains.

Delabole's men scurried in and out, ferrying in the monitoring equipment, testing it, making interminable minor adjustments. To add to the chaotic scene other officers were bringing in desks, chairs, typewriters, telephones, beds, bedclothes, food, and amongst it all Corelli wandered from room to room questioning, issuing orders, mentally ticking off the items as they arrived.

Dice had looked in, then left Corelli to it, retiring to the command van where comparative peace and quiet was to be found.

When some semblance of order had been achieved Corelli called him up on the jury-rigged telephone line.

Dice entered the room and went straight to the telescope. He was looking down on the siege flat which was at an angle to his right. But this position of advantage availed him little. Heavy curtains were drawn across the fixed window and through the long net curtains on the french windows he had only a blurred impression of the front corner of the kitchen area. He could see no movement.

He crossed to the officer sitting at a desk in front of a radio receiver, insulated by earphones from the noise of the room. He tapped him on the shoulder.

'Turn it up, son,' he said.

'Not a sound so far, sir,' said the officer, turning up the volume.

Dice nodded and turned to Corelli.

'Where's the television monitor?'

Dead on cue Delabole entered trailing a scattering of acolytes. One of them held the monitor, the others were laying the cables.

'Where d'you want it, old chap?' Delabole asked Dice.

'On the desk here, sir,' Corelli said.

The monitor was positioned, the cables arranged along the wall. Delabole switched on at the socket, then played with the controls of the monitor. The picture jumped and flickered, then settled down. The definition was indifferent but quite adequate for the purpose.

The watching officers could see most of the kitchen area, the entrance door blocked by two desks, and perhaps a half of the living area including a settee and two armchairs. A man was lounging in one of the armchairs, a Kalashnikov automatic rifle in his hands. On the floor in front of the barricaded door, almost in the centre of the picture, were the two hostages, bound and gagged and lying facing each other. It was impossible to say if they were alive or dead.

'Not a bad picture, eh?' said Delabole into the silence.

A girl entered their vision, walking across the room from the living area to stand beside the man. She was slim, dark haired, smartly dressed, attractive, and she also carried a Kalashnikov rifle loosely in her hands.

'Can you get me a still shot of them, blow it up for me?' Dice asked Delabole.

'Certainly.'

'Give a copy to Colin Land as soon as you can. Maybe Special Branch can identify them.'

'Will do.'

An officer took over control of the monitor and Delabole left. Dice stood for a long while staring at the screen, then he went to one wall where Corelli had fixed a pegboard sheet on which were maps of Hampstead, the siege building and the siege flat. The latter had furniture marked in position in the siege room.

Dice checked the furniture plan against what he could see on the monitor. It seemed that only the desks barricading the door had been moved.

Corelli had left with Delabole. He came back into the room with an army officer and two sergeants. All three were armed and looked as if they had been struck from the same granite mould.

'This is Lieutenant Bannister, S.A.S., sir,' said Corelli. 'Commander Dice,' he added for Bannister's benefit.

The two men acknowledged each other.

'How many men do you have?' Dice asked.

'Twelve. I can call on more if needed.'

'We have worked out suggested dispositions for your men. Let Mr Corelli know if you decide to make any changes, would you?'

'Of course. What weapons have they?'

'Kalashnikov automatic rifles. Probably explosives and hand guns.'

'You don't plan any positive action?'

'No. We play the waiting game.'

Bannister seemed fractionally disappointed.

'One last thing,' said Dice. 'No one fires a single shot without direct orders from Mr Corelli or myself.'

'Understood.'

'Glad to have you with us, Mr Bannister.'

Bannister and Dice shook hands, then Corelli led the army men out of the room.

Dice went to the window and looked out. Officers were completing a sandbag wall behind the wooden shutters in front of the siege building, against the possibility of an explosion inside the flat. Others would be doing the same inside the flat and in the hallway of the building.

A bank of powerful arc lights were in position, pointing directly at the windows of the siege flat, and officers were clustered about them, adjusting angles, laying out cables. Further down the road, behind the end barricades, there was a cough of black smoke, a clattering rumble as the diesel engine of the generator burst into life. It ran for a few moments, then stopped, the test complete.

Dice looked at his watch. Incredibly it was still only 2 p.m. On the television monitor screen nothing had changed. The hostages had made slight movements, they were still alive. The terrorists seemed relaxed, indifferent. They had not spoken a word.

Inspector Beal telephoned from the command van, asked for Dice.

'We have a message from "ED", sir. They arrested a tramp this morning, man named Thomas Bowler, in possession of a W.P.C.'s uniform and some other female clothing.'

'Yes?'

'It might tie in with message fifteen from D.A.C. Cottar, the one reporting the two P.C.s on the front entrance to the Yard as recording a W.P.C. taking the wrong lift to "A" Department.'

'Has he said anything, the tramp?'

'Says he nicked the stuff from a car in Camden Town, sir.'

'Do they have the car?'

'Yes, sir.'

'Are you free, David? Can you go and see him?'

'Yes, sir.'

'Do that. If it looks right, inform Mr Corelli, he'll arrange for the circus to look over the vehicle.'

Dice found himself a chair and sat watching the monitor screen. The man was still lounging in an armchair, the girl prowling about the room, apparently searching cupboards. After a while she walked up behind the armchair, leant over and whispered into the man's ear.

So, they had anticipated a listening device. And what else? What else had they anticipated, planned for?

The question was unanswerable but it nagged at him constantly throughout the afternoon.

20 At 5 p.m. the girl switched on the radio and tuned in to the news broadcast. They were the big story. The Commissioner of Police had a strong, deep brown voice. He said that the terrorists were trapped, that they had no hope, that eventually they would have to give themselves up. He appealed to them, if they were listening, to do so.

The terrorists exchanged grins.

They learnt just two things from the broadcast. That a Commander Dice was in charge of the case and that the police had called in the S.A.S.

The newscaster passed on to other items. The girl switched off the radio.

'They can stuff Dice and his S.A.S.,' she said aloud, for the benefit of the listeners. 'You hear me, Dice? First sign we see of the bloody S.A.S. we shoot one of the hostages.'

'In the guts,' her partner added.

The girl felt relaxed and confident. It was going well. The reality had so far turned out so much easier than the training. Unlike the stinking hot, bug-ridden hut in Cuba, this room was clean, light and airy. They had bedding, and water, food, and they were well armed. And there were no sadistic instructors sneering at every tiny slip, no barrage of capitalist propaganda hammering at their eardrums until they were desperate for quiet, no prying television camera watching them scratch, urinate, sweat or vent their lust. This time they would not be tried to breaking point. This was the real thing. They were on their own, free agents, the job almost complete.

She felt a surge of pride. They had already succeeded, no matter what happened now their mission would be complete. And they would go free, of that she was sure.

The man came across to her and whispered in her ear. 'I'm hungry.'

'Okay. Get us some food. Use what's in the fridge first.'

'What about them?'

He pointed at the hostages.

'Better give them something.'

He went to the kitchen area. The girl knelt down beside the hostages, spoke out loud.

'I'm going to take off your gags, undo your hands. If you make one wrong move, speak one word, you're dead. Get that? Say one word and you're dead.'

She removed the gags, untied their hands and pushed them up into a sitting position.

The hostages stretched themselves carefully, trying out cramped limbs and stiffened face muscles. Mary Tü fixed her eyes on Paul Carpenter's face. He forced a determined smile for her sake. But she had heard on the radio, as he had, of the death of Alex Pope, and silent, hopeless tears followed each other down her face.

Carpenter touched her hand briefly, hoping to give her strength but bitterly aware of his own fears.

The man put food and two cups of water down on the floor between them, then he and the girl sat in the armchairs, eating and watching their hostages.

Mary Tü made no move to eat or drink. Paul crossed himself, closed his eyes briefly in prayer, then put food in her mouth, raised the cup to her lips.

Then Mary understood that this was an act of communion,

an act private between her and Paul, her priest, an act which the terrorists would not understand. He was telling her, have faith. She smiled her understanding, her belief.

'Ain't that sweet!' said the man, in ignorance.

The girl put her fingers to her lips, cautioning him. She pointed at Carpenter, made an obscene gesture including the girl. The man snickered and repeated the gesture.

When they had eaten they bound and gagged the hostages again. The man urinated loudly and obviously into the sink. The girl picked a book from a shelf and leafed through it. The title was *The Post Industrial Society*. Now and then she giggled to herself at the political naïvety of the contents.

The hostages were lying a foot apart, face to face. Mary Tü was momentarily at peace, fortified by the improvised sacrament. The priest closed his eyes, prayed hard, seeking a respite from the destructive, demoralizing fear that possessed him.

21 Dice sat transfixed in front of the television monitor screen for several hours, studying every movement, every gesture the terrorists made.

He was relieved when the hostages were given food and water but saw in it no weakening of the terrorists' resolve. For the time being they needed the hostages alive. He recognized the significance of the priest's silent help for Mary Tü, admired his bravery, but prayed that Carpenter would, if only for the girl's sake, do nothing to antagonize his captors.

At 7 p.m. the hourly megaphone contact was made, relayed over the microphone link to the control flat. It had an unexpected effect on the girl terrorist. She became suddenly agitated, grabbing up her gun and running across the room to the door.

Her voice was harsh and loud in the control flat because of her proximity to the microphone on the door. On the screen Dice could see that her face was contorted in violent anger.

'Stop that you bastards, you hear me?'

Then she fired at the door, a single shot angled down the

passage. The noise of the shot reverberated round the control flat, hammering at the ears of the officers, shocking them momentarily. The girl had intended to kill.

'Get me Chief Inspector Kent on the landline immediately,' said Dice.

'Use that thing once more and I'll shoot one of the hostages, right?' shouted the girl.

'Mr Kent, cancel use of the megaphone pending further orders,' said Dice into the landline receiver.

He watched the girl return to her armchair, drop the automatic rifle on the floor beside her. The man had not moved throughout. Now he looked at her and they exchanged a grin. They seemed relaxed, unconcerned.

Dice was worried by the incident. It had seemed initially to be spontaneous, now he was sure it was not. They had coldly planned to dispense with the annoyance of the loudhailer, had been prepared to kill to make their point. Without the benefit of the T.V. camera this would not have been obvious, it would have seemed a genuine, almost predictable outburst. Perhaps it was that the terrorists were not particularly concerned about the loudhailer but were simply giving the police what they expected. It was that thought which most worried Dice.

Some time later Chief Superintendent Corelli came into the room accompanied by Detective Inspector Beal. Corelli indicated that Beal should tell his story first.

'This tramp, sir, the stolen police uniform,' Beal began.

'Yes?' Dice enquired.

'He saw the changeover of cars. He stole the uniform with some other clothes from the car they used for the Pope killing, saw them take off in the 15-cwt van.'

'And how did they get hold of the uniform?'

'It was stolen during a break-in at a W.P.C.'s private flat in Wimbledon four days ago.'

'Which solves the problem of how they got into the Yard,' commented Corelli.

'Did he see any weapons, explosives?' Dice asked.

'No, sir. But he said they took away two holdalls. They seemed fairly heavy.'

'Did he hear them talking?'

'Yes. But he says he was too far away to understand what they were saying.'

'They were speaking English?'

'He thought so.'

'He'll be kept in custody?'

'Yes, sir. If we need him he'll be around. Got a string as long as his arm, bound to get six months anyway.'

'Thank you, David, you can carry on here now.'

Corelli took over.

'The matter of the food they have available.'

'Yes?'

'The old lady downstairs says Carpenter last went shopping three days ago. He had two plastic carrier bags; one was full and there were fresh vegetables on the top; the other was half full but we don't know what he bought.'

'Where does he do his shopping?'

'Supermarket in the High Street, but they can't remember. Not surprising really. Anyway, there can't be all that much left, unless his secretary brought some in and the old lady doesn't think so.'

'Whilst I think of it, Ray. We have kept in touch with Carpenter's relatives, haven't we, and the girl's, what's her name again?'

'Mary Tü. Yes sir, we give them regular bulletins.'

Dice changed tack again.

'So they will probably go hungry in a couple of days, surprising.'

Corelli looked puzzled.

'What's surprising about that, sir?'

'Not that they will go hungry, but that they should have fed the hostages today, and fairly liberally too. What else have you for me?'

'I've just spoken to Mr Peach at C.3. He had several good

sets of prints on the van we recovered here. At the moment he's getting elimination prints from the owners and the driver. It's owned by a small delivery firm, stolen yesterday from their depot.'

'When will he be finished?'

'He won't say, sir. I think in the morning.'

'Put him on to the car they used for the Pope murder.'

'Yes, sir.'

'And get David to arrange for the girl's clothing we recovered to go to the lab.'

'That's been done, sir. Anything else?'

'When you've done that you can come back here. We'll watch television.'

Corelli grinned but Dice had already returned to his seat in front of the monitor.

The terrorists read books taken from Carpenter's collection, then they produced a pack of cards and began to play poker, using matches in lieu of money.

At 9 p.m. Dice telephoned his home. He let it ring for a long time but there was no answer. Then he returned to his seat in front of the monitor.

Corelli studiously ignored Dice's brief absence from his seat. Corelli hated Betty Dice, hated her for what she was doing to her husband. He could not understand how Dice tolerated it.

22 The girl took a blank sheet of typing paper from Carpenter's desk and wrote on it the days of the week. Then she crossed off Monday and Tuesday.

She switched on the radio and they waited for the 10 p.m. news bulletin. They corrected their watches against the time signal then listened to the first part of the bulletin, that relating to the siege. It was virtually a repeat of the earlier bulletin except that they now had quotes from members of the hostages' family and senior members of the Christian Democrat Party. The girl switched off when the newsreader changed the subject.

The man crossed to the hostages, bent close to Carpenter, spoke quietly into his ear.

'You want the can?'

Carpenter stared at him blankly.

'You want to piss? Nod your head. You can use the sink.'

Carpenter looked across at the sink, then shook his head.

'You?'

Mary Tü shook her head.

The man returned to speak to the girl.

'They're holding it,' he whispered, 'don't want to do it in public.'

'Nor do I. We'll get something sent in.'

'When?'

'Later. When they're not expecting it.'

They returned to a disinterested study of Carpenter's books. At 11 p.m. the girl collected the blankets she had taken from the bedroom, threw one over the hostages, then covered herself up on an armchair and went to sleep.

The man sat in the other armchair, his automatic rifle in his lap. He remained awake.

23 'They were very interested in the news bulletin,' Corelli commented.

He and Dice were alone in the room apart from the two officers operating the monitoring equipment.

'Were they? Or were they just interested in the time signal?' said Dice.

'Both, perhaps.'

'Perhaps.'

'I don't see why the exact time should interest them. It's not as if they were going anywhere.'

'They might think they are.'

'You think they'll try to barter for an aircraft?'

'They might.'

'They must know we wouldn't agree.'

'Perhaps they have an ace up their sleeve.'

'Like what?'

'I don't know.'

Corelli changed his position on the hard chair. There was no action on the screen. The hostages lay still, the girl was apparently asleep, the man keeping watch. Now and then he yawned but there was no sign that he might himself fall asleep.

'I'd like to know what she wrote on that piece of paper,' Dice said.

'Perhaps she's keeping a diary.'

'It might be something like that.'

Corelli was surprised.

'I was joking. She just wrote a few words in a single column, that's what it looked like anyway, then she went back to the beginning and crossed out the first two or three.'

Dice clicked his fingers, signalling an idea.

'Monday and Tuesday,' he said.

'Eh?'

'I think she wrote down the days of the week, then crossed off Monday and Tuesday.'

'Why?'

'I don't know. If they anticipate a long siege they may be establishing a time-based routine. It helps to maintain a psychological balance, avoid disorientation.'

'Yes, of course.'

They watched in silence for a moment. The microphone was producing a low purring sound. The girl was snoring gently.

'They speak good English,' said Corelli.

'Yes.'

'Even amongst themselves.'

'We don't know that. We've only heard a few words, under stress.'

'The tramp said they did.'

'He thought so.'

'And the whispering, somehow even that sounds British.'

'You may be right. I don't think they originate from this country though.'

At midnight the telephone rang suddenly, startling them. The officer who answered almost sat to attention, offered the receiver to Dice.

'The Commissioner, sir.'

Sir John Cowling had telephoned each hour since he had left the scene.

'Anything new, Allan?' he asked.

'No, sir. They've bedded down for the night.'

'You'll contact me, no matter what time, if anything happens.'

'Yes, sir.'

'Good night, Allan.'

'Good night, sir.'

Dice waited until the line had cleared then dialled his home number. He waited, but there was no reply. He put down the receiver and resumed his seat.

'I'll stay, sir. You could nip off home for a few hours,' Corelli said, not looking at Dice.

'No, Ray. Perhaps tomorrow. I stay here tonight. You go, come back at seven.'

'If anything . . .'

'I'll call you out. I'd need you.'

At 1 a.m. Dice retired to the next-door room where a bed had been made up. He stripped naked and knelt beside the bed, head bowed.

He prayed for help, for guidance. He prayed for his wife, for Corelli, for Sir John Cowling. He prayed especially for the hostages and for the terrorists. That last was the hardest of all.

Then he slept.

WEDNESDAY

24 CODE: SK.10.F. FROM DIAKENOV EXECUTIVE ACTION DEPARTMENT 1ST CHIEF EXECUTIVE TO MAZTIKYAN LONDON REFERENTURA. EXPECT KARELIN (E.A.D.) AEROFLOT 259 THURSDAY. COVER CULTURAL ATTACHE. PRIORITY MISSION REPORTING THIS OFFICE ONLY. ASSIST AS REQUESTED. DESTRUCT NOTICE APPLIES. END.

25 Corelli arrived at 7 a.m. and found Dice watching the television monitor.

'All quiet on the western front, sir?' he asked.

'They slept like babies,' said Dice.

On the screen the girl was still asleep in the armchair, the man awake, cuddling his Kalashnikov rifle. The hostages seemed not to have moved.

'He must be feeling it by now,' said Corelli.

'They took three-hour shifts.'

Corelli put a bundle of files down on a desk.

'I collected these on the way in. Our files on the Christian Democrat Party and reports from the hostages' doctors.'

Dice came across to the desk, sat down and started with the doctors' reports.

'Have you had breakfast, sir?' Corelli asked.

'No.'

'I'll have a word with Mr Peach, see if he's isolated the fingerprints, bring some food up with me if you'd like.'

Dice was immersed in his reading.

'Fine.'

Corelli was gone for an hour. He returned with a covered breakfast tray, placed it on a table in a corner of the room. Dice was watching the monitor.

The girl was awake but showed no signs of moving from the chair. The man got up, checked the hostages, nodded to the girl and sat down again.

'They're alive anyway,' said Corelli.

Dice got up and inspected the food. He indicated for Corelli to join him.

'Get a cup of coffee, come and talk to me,' he said.

When they were settled Corelli began by repeating his conversation with Commander Peach.

'He's isolated the prints. One set male, one set female, obviously the villains.'

'And?'

'No trace.'

Dice did not seem surprised.

'He's given a copy to Special Branch and Interpol?' he asked.

'Yes. It'll take time for them to report back though, maybe more time than we've got.'

'We have to know who they are, Ray, and soon.'

'Yes.'

'Strange no one has claimed responsibility yet.'

'No doubt they will, they're getting world-wide publicity, what use if they don't put their name to it?'

'Exactly.'

No more was said until Dice had finished eating. Then he sipped at his coffee and looked at Corelli over the rim of his cup.

'We have to get the hostages untied,' he said.

'I didn't have a chance to read the doctors' reports.'

'It's not that. They're healthy enough. Carpenter hasn't been to his doctor for a year, Mary Tü not for three years and that was only for the cure.'

'The cure?'

'Venereal disease.'

'Good God!'

Corelli was genuinely shocked.

'It's in the file, twelve cons. She was on the game until she met Carpenter, found Christ.'

'I didn't know, I didn't expect that . . .'

'It makes no difference.'

'If the press got hold of it they'd crucify her.'

Dice smiled wanly.

'Sometimes your choice of phrase is a little doubtful, Ray,' he said.

Corelli flushed.

'I mean, somehow you don't expect an ex-pro to be involved with men like Pope and Carpenter . . . men of the Church, so to speak.'

'There are precedents,' said Dice dryly.

Corelli collected himself.

'But they're not going to need medical attention?'

'No. But I want them untied, as fit as possible, just in case.'

Corelli shook his head.

'What can we do? They don't want to negotiate.'

'They will soon.'

'I don't see why. They've got food, water, they can stick it out for a week.'

'They can't cook, and food must be short, but despite that they're not conserving it. They intend to negotiate.'

'Perhaps,' said Corelli, doubtfully.

'I intend to have a landline dropped down on to the balcony,' said Dice, 'make it easy for them.'

'Shall I speak to Mr Delabole, arrange it?'

'No hurry. He'll be here later this morning.'

Corelli finished his coffee.

'I'll go and see how David Beal is getting on in the command van.'

'Whilst you're there, Ray, phone Tickner and Peck, ask them to come at their early convenience.'

When Corelli had gone Dice telephoned the Commissioner but had little to report.

26 At 9 a.m. the girl switched on the radio and they checked their watches, then listened to the news bulletin. They were still prime news but there was an obvious shortage of fresh copy.

Afterwards the man checked the stock of food. He whispered in the girl's ear.

'There's only enough for one meal.'

'Then we eat tonight.'

'I'm hungry now.'

She looked at him angrily.

'Live with it. Drink water.'

He jerked his thumb at the hostages.

'We could get two meals if we leave them out.'

'They get fed,' she said flatly.

'Hell, why? We're going to . . .'

'We came here to execute two class traitors. We didn't come here to torture them, starve them.'

'What the hell does it matter?'

She turned on him, eyes blazing.

'I wonder about you sometimes, I wonder just how deep your commitment is.'

The man bridled.

'That's bloody unfair. My record's as good as yours.'

'Then keep it that way. Untie them, give them water, let them exercise, but make sure they keep quiet.'

He untied and ungagged the hostages.

'Not a word,' he whispered fiercely at them.

He brought them water, and they drank. He watched them flex cramped muscles, gave them five minutes, then tied and gagged them again.

The girl was standing by the french windows, looking out across the road. He came to join her.

'I think they're in that top flat,' she whispered, pointing.

'Looks empty,' he said.

'It's where I'd be.'

'Makes no difference.'

'No.'

'I've been thinking.'

'Really?'

'If we were to make contact we could get some food, and a toilet.'

'No!'

'Why not? I'm hungry and I'm bursting to go, you must be too.'

'Sit on it, or go in a corner.'

'And use what?'

'Imagination.'

'You're making it hard for us, why not talk, get what we want?'

'We must keep the initiative. Contact is a weapon, we'll use it to best advantage, when they're least expecting it.'

He lapsed into a sulky silence.

Then, as they stared out of the window the landline telephone appeared in sight, the handpiece taped to the body of the receiver, turned gently on its own umbilical cord, settling gently on the floor of the balcony.

'Hell!' whispered the man. 'They must've heard us.'

'No,' she said, 'he's just good, bloody good.'

'Who?'

'Dice. He said his name was Dice.'

The landline telephone on the balcony began to ring.

27 Dice telephoned his home number. It was two minutes before his wife answered. Her voice was slurred with sleep. She repeated the number.

'Betty, it's Dice.'

'Oh, yes . . .'

'You know what's happening?'

'Er, yes, I heard on the radio, I guessed . . .'

Her voice tailed off, he could hear her yawning.

'Are you all right?'

'Yes, fine.'

'I'll try to get back tonight.'

'Okay.'

'You know how it is.'

'Yes.'

'You'll be there, tonight?'

'Don't know.'

'Try.'

'Okay.'

'Goodbye, dear.'

'Bye, Dice.'

Dice replaced the receiver as Corelli entered the command room with Doctor Tickner.

'Thought you'd be after me,' said Tickner, extending his hand to Dice.

'Who else?' said Dice.

They had been in this situation together before, neither felt any need to stand on ceremony.

'Any medical problems?'

'No. We have a report from the hostages' G.P.s.'

'This going to be a long one?'

'I think so.'

'I'll make myself comfortable then.'

'I'll get another monitor sent in, run the tape through for you up to date.'

'Fine. Any coffee going?'

'Mr Delabole is in the command van, sir,' said Corelli, 'he's sending up another monitor and the tapes.'

'You have a psychiatrist coming?' asked Tickner.

'Yes. Jean Peck,' Dice answered.

'She'll do. Nice boobs, Jean. Have you noticed how most female psychiatrists are flat chested?'

'I can't say I have,' said Dice.

'Maybe I've just been unlucky,' said Tickner. 'I won't run the tape until she comes.'

Corelli brought him coffee, sat him at a free table.

Commander Delabole entered carrying an envelope. Behind him came two detectives carrying the heavy equipment. As they set it up on Tickner's table, Delabole handed the envelope to Dice.

'Portraits of your villains, Dice,' he said.

Dice looked at them. They were better than he had expected.

'Good morning, Mike.'

'Morning,' said Delabole, 'how's things?'

'So so. Has Colin Land got a copy of these?'

'Yes, old thing, and Interpol.'

'Did Colin say anything?'

'He said thank you.'

A telephone bell rang. Corelli answered it.

Doctor Jean Peck was ushered into the room by Detective Inspector Beal. Dice smiled a greeting.

'Jean . . .'

'Hullo Dice.'

Her voice was warm and husky, her figure merited Tickner's appreciation. She greeted no one else, somehow excluded them simply by fixing her eyes on Dice's face.

'Lovely to see you,' said Dice.

'After such a long time,' she added.

She thought he looked older, tired. There was more grey at the temples, a darkness under the eyes. But he was still Dice, still slim and neat, still cool and patrician, still remote, unobtainable.

'So glad you could come to help us out,' he said.

'A pleasure, Dice. You know that.'

Corelli replaced the receiver, noted the interplay. You're wasting your time, girl, he thought, he doesn't even know what you're up to.

Dice led her to a chair beside Tickner, sat her down. Corelli came up behind him.

'That was the lab, sir.'

'Yes?'

'There's a ream of stuff coming on the two vehicles and contents but I doubt it will tell us anything new.'

Dice nodded.

Corelli looked round the room.

'Well, the gang's all here,' he said.

'So they are,' said Dice.

'Shall I try the landline again?' Corelli asked.

'If you like.'

'You don't sound enthusiastic, sir.'

'They won't answer yet,' said Dice.

28 Paul Carpenter moved, rolled gently over on to his back.

His spine was now arched over his bound arms but it eased the pain across his shoulder blades that had become almost unbearable in the last hour.

His left arm and left leg felt numb apart from a distant prickling sensation. He was beginning to be conscious of hunger and worst of all was the urgent need to use a toilet. His stomach felt at once empty and blown out.

He turned his head to look at Mary Tü. For once she was looking away from him. He knew she must be suffering equal discomfort. It worried him, angered him that he could do nothing for her.

Why did she have to be here? Why had God allowed it? This was not her fight. He had recognized that this could happen to him. A Christian is for ever under siege, it was never an easy life, and if you join battle with evil forces you can expect to face extreme persecution.

He had dedicated his life to Christ and he would die for his belief if need be, but in the meantime why did Mary have to be here and why was he unable to put from his mind the desperate need for such a mundane physical act as the use of a toilet?

Surely martyrdom, if that was his lot, should have a greater aura of dignity?

It did not seem much to ask. He was a fool. Why had he not gone into the corner when they gave him the opportunity?

Then, with blinding suddenness, he recognized the carping cadences of self-pity. He was horrified, ashamed of himself, aware of his failure.

Of all people he should have known that he could do nothing for himself, nothing without God. Was his faith after all so weak, he who had dared to attempt to change the social structure of a whole nation, orientate it towards his own belief?

This was his trial. It was God's will that Mary Tü should be a witness, perhaps even make her own sacrifice. His sin was grievous, it burdened him far beyond his physical discomfort. He prayed for forgiveness.

Into his mind came the comforting and inspiring words at the end of Christ's Sermon on the Mount . . . 'How blest you are, when you suffer insults and persecution and every kind of calumny for my sake. Accept it with gladness and exultation, for you have a rich reward in heaven; in the same way they persecuted the prophets before you.'

And the priest knew he was forgiven. He knew that he was going to die, he saw the absolute necessity for it.

And he was, for the moment, at peace.

29 Dice was talking on the telephone in the command flat, talking to Commander Land, Special Branch.

'It takes time, Dice,' Land said.

'You have photographs, fingerprints, how much time?'

'Nobody has claimed responsibility, we have a wide field to cover.'

'It's important, Colin.'

'I know.'

'When they make contact I want to know who I'm dealing with. You understand it might make the difference between success and disaster?'

'Half-baked information won't help, Dice. Nor will guesses.'

'You could make a guess?'

'I could, but I'm not going to.'

'If you need the co-operation of the Security Services I'm sure it could be arranged at top level.'

'It's already been done, Dice. Go away, leave me in peace, when I have something concrete you'll be first to know.'

Dice replaced the receiver. Corelli stood at his shoulder.

'No go, sir?' Corelli asked.

'Not yet,' said Dice.

They stood leaning on the backs of chairs, watching the monitor. The hostages occasionally made slight movements. The terrorists were playing cards.

At 11 a.m. the Commissioner entered the room and buttonholed Dice.

'I have a press conference in half an hour, Allan. Do we have anything new for them?'

'You could tell them we've called in a doctor and a psychiatrist, sir.'

'Yes, fine . . .'

'You have seen the photographs we lifted from the television tape?'

'Yes, quite good.'

'I thought you could make an appeal for aid from the press, try to identify them. They must have been in this country for several days, they must have stayed somewhere.'

'Yes. Appeal to hotels, landladies, that sort of thing.'

'Yes, sir.'

'The press will need the photographs.'

'We can't give them the photographs, but I've had excellent photofit likenesses made up from them. The press can have those.'

'Why not the real thing? Surely . . .'

'The terrorists might wonder where we got the photographs from. We can't risk them finding the T.V. camera.'

'Hell! Of course not.'

Corelli handed over an envelope.

'The photofit pictures, sir.'

'Thank you, Corelli.'

'You know our doctors of course, sir,' said Dice.

The Commissioner greeted Tickner and Peck.

'Are we looking after you?' he enquired amiably.

'You are,' said Tickner.

'We've become old hands at this,' said Jean Peck.

'What do you think of them?' Sir John asked, pointing vaguely in the direction of the monitor.

'Healthy animals, the lot of them,' said Tickner, 'but I'd be happier if the hostages weren't tied up like chickens.'

'Yes.'

The Commissioner looked enquiringly at the psychiatrist.

'I can't tell about the hostages. The terrorists seem calm. There is no apparent likelihood of an immediate outburst, but the potential for violence is obviously there.'

'You think we might be here for some time?'

'It looks like it.'

Sir John Cowling stared thoughtfully at the monitor screen. He would have preferred a different answer but he was far too experienced an officer to attempt to push any of these people. Better a long siege ending successfully than a short one ending in a bloody confrontation. Politically, the latter possibility was disastrous.

'I must leave you now,' he said. 'Anything you need, Allan?'

'Not for the moment, sir,' said Dice.

After the Commissioner had gone Dice and Corelli sat down to watch the monitor.

'I wouldn't have thought Carpenter had much time for playing cards,' Corelli commented after a moment.

'I think they brought the pack with them,' said Dice.

30 Sir John Cowling had a lunch appointment with the Home Secretary. The meeting was cordial but cool. No word of criticism was uttered but the Commissioner left with the clear impression that more was expected of him than he had so far produced.

The newspapers were rightly pointing out that the Pope killing was a direct blow at British democracy. They were screaming at the Government, baying for some positive action from the uncertain and reluctant politicians, speculating wildly about which political grouping might be responsible for the atrocity. Alexander Pope had been built up into a folk hero by the media, he regularly received more coverage for himself, and his party, than the other three parties put together. Everything he said in life was news, in death he had assumed supernatural powers. The will of the British people, as voiced by the fourth estate, was for revenge, for action, for a general election.

The Home Secretary needed results from the Commissioner. He subtly suggested a harder line should be taken in this siege, not actually saying that some degree of violence would be acceptable, but leaving Sir John Cowling in no doubt that provided Carpenter lived, chances might justifiably be taken with the lives of others. He said that, but were his words to be repeated out of the context of the meeting they would be open to other, more orthodox interpretations. The Home Secretary had left himself ample space for manoeuvre.

As his car whisked him across London, back to New Scotland Yard, the Commissioner had much to think about. What he was being asked to do went against his convictions as a policeman and might be personally damaging if a stronger line produced a violent reaction.

The attack on the Yard was a severe dent in the façade of near-invincibility that his force had long enjoyed in matters of major crime. Now Pope was dead and Carpenter a hostage. The onus for action, for saving Carpenter's life, was upon *him*. He was acutely aware that he was vulnerable. If he failed then his own political ambitions outside the force were ended for ever. And those ambitions had now to be revised. None of the established political parties could now confidently anticipate victory in an election. The Christian Democrat Party had the money and the necessary organization to put up candidates in every ward. If they did so the emotional tide following the Pope killing might just sweep them into power.

Sir John Cowling had not yet chosen his political horse. He had had in mind to commit himself to the party presently in power, now he must think again. Perhaps he would have a more certain ride with the Christian Democrats when the dust of this affair had settled.

It mattered that he make an early decision. He could bow to the Home Secretary's wishes, push Dice into harsher, perhaps precipitant action. If he did that and Carpenter died, he alone would carry the can and his chances of political advancement with the Christian Democrats would be nil. If he let things take their course and the Government suffered because of it, then he could look for no political help in that direction.

He had to decide now.

When he returned to his office he found Assistant Commissioner Cottar waiting in the ante-room.

'You want to see me, Reg?'

'Yes, sir. If you have a moment.'

'A moment, yes.'

The Commissioner sat at his desk, left Cottar standing. He found his senior officer's gross figure vaguely offensive, his constant sniffing an irritant.

'It's about the Spencer Street siege, sir.'

'Yes?'

'I'm a little concerned about it.'

'So are we all.'

'I wonder if Dice is really the man for this particular job?'

'We sent him to America, Israel, Europe, studying siege situations. He has successfully concluded three similar cases in the last four years. He lectures on the subject at our training schools. He is the author of our instruction manual and operations procedure for siege incidents. His service record is impeccable. You have some complaint of him?'

Cottar changed his ground rapidly.

'No, sir, naturally not. It's a matter of personality and relates only to this case.'

'What, then?'

'He is a religious man, of course . . .'

Having cast his bread, Cottar hesitated, waiting for a reaction.

'So?'

'That might incline him to the soft approach, a turning of the cheek . . .'

'Our policy is, and always has been, the soft approach. It works.'

'Quite, sir, but this case I suggest is different. It has enormous political implications. Perhaps our political masters might appreciate a somewhat more definite approach.'

Suspicion wormed its way into the Commissioner's mind. Was it pure chance that Cottar was parroting the words he had heard so recently from the lips of the Home Secretary?

'As you know, sir, Dice is an uncommunicative sort of chap, short on words. That doesn't go down well with the press and we need them on our side,' Cottar continued. 'Then, of course, you know he has trouble with that wife of his . . .'

'I know.'

'We couldn't take the chance that his mind was not on the job one hundred per cent.'

'What do you suggest, Reg?' asked the Commissioner silkily.

Cottar was more relaxed now. The interview was proving to be easier than he had expected.

'You might consider, sir, that an officer of higher rank should be placed in executive charge of this operation. No public reflection on Dice of course, simply because of the particularly delicate political nature of this enquiry.'

So, there it was. Cottar wanted the centre role. And what else he might want thereafter was self evident. He was a man of unbounded ambition. And Cottar had high-placed contacts, he had been primed to make this approach, so aptly timed as it was. Someone in the political hierarchy had a more malleable commissioner in mind, that much was clear.

Sir John Cowling sat back in his chair and looked amiably at his brother officer, his decision made.

'That would present me with a problem, Reg,' he said blandly.

'I don't see why, sir.'

'I have no officer senior in rank to Dice who is more competent than he in this kind of case.'

It was a blunt and vicious rebuff, a throwing down of the gauntlet. A handkerchief appeared magically in Cottar's hand. His hay fever had suddenly come on again.

31 At 6 p.m. the girl switched on the transistor radio and checked her watch against the time signal. Then they listened to the news.

The police had called in a doctor and a psychiatrist. They had photofit likenesses of the two terrorists and were trying to identify them, find out where they had been staying since they arrived in England. The Commissioner said he was confident of ultimate success.

The girl switched off the radio. There was nothing in the broadcast to concern her unduly.

The man brought in the remainder of the food and they split it into four portions. The girl untied the hostages, warned them to silence, then watched them as they moved heavy limbs, massaged cramped muscles.

She admitted to a sneaking admiration for the way they had accepted their capture. She was well aware of the shock effect of sudden violence, it had been part of her training, but these two were standing up to their ordeal better than most. She thought she knew why. Like her they had a belief, an ideal to cling to, to draw strength from. It was the lack of a belief, of an ideal, that made the bulk of the proletariat of the capitalist world so malleable, so vulnerable.

When they had eaten she took old newspapers from a kitchen

drawer, spread them on the floor in a corner and pulled across an armchair to provide a modicum of privacy. She and the man used this primitive facility first, then she allowed Carpenter and the girl to follow them.

Mary Tü looked at Carpenter for guidance. He nodded his head, then went into the corner.

Afterwards the girl went close up to Carpenter and whispered fiercely in his ear.

'Pick it up.'

She pointed to the corner.

'Throw it out of the window, into the street.'

She stood by the french windows, held them open as Carpenter hurled the bundle into the street, then nudged him back into the room with her gun.

Carpenter pointed to the table, to a pencil and paper the terrorists had used to keep score in one of their interminable card games. He looked enquiringly at her.

The girl hesitated momentarily, then nodded.

Carpenter wrote quickly on the paper, handed it to her. She read: 'In God's name do not tie my secretary up again.'

The girl threw the paper down and jammed the barrel of her rifle into Carpenter's stomach. He doubled up, the air gushing from his lungs.

When both the hostages were tied and gagged the girl handed the paper Carpenter had written on to her partner. He read it, grinned at her, struck a match on the table top and set fire to the paper, holding it until the flame burnt his fingers.

32 'What do you make of that, Jean?' Dice asked.

Everyone in the command flat had been glued to the monitor for the last half-hour.

The psychiatrist continued to stare at the screen.

'They seem very sure of themselves,' she said.

'Why the violence? Why feed the hostages, have some care for their well-being, then resort to sudden, needless violence?'

'They enjoy it,' said Tickner. 'Bullies love dishing it out when the victim can't hit back.'

'There's more to it than that,' said Dice.

'They're not just physical bullies,' said Corelli, 'they're ideological bullies as well. The sort that'd put razor blades in a playground slide and make out it was for the good of mankind.'

Jean Peck looked across to Dice.

'Dice, there's something wrong here,' she said.

'I know. What?'

'I'm not sure.'

On the screen the girl was doing calisthenic exercises whilst the man kept guard.

'Guess,' Dice suggested.

'Everything they do suggests confidence, and I'm sure it's not put on. It's as if . . . Dice, you have this area surrounded, they can't possibly get away, can they?'

'I don't think so.'

'And no one could get in to rescue them?'

'I very much doubt it.'

'Then it makes no sense because I suspect that they think they're going to escape. I think they imagine they've already beaten you.'

'Yes,' said Dice, 'I'm sure they think that.'

After fifteen minutes the girl took over guard and the man went through the exercise routine. Then they began playing cards.

Daylight failed just after 9 p.m. and the floodlights came on. The man drew the curtains in the siege flat and the girl took a blanket and went to sleep in an armchair.

Dice had a headache. Corelli fetched aspirin and Dice retired to his bedroom for a while.

He lay on the bed, felt under the pillow and retrieved his Bible, opened it at random. He read from Chapter 12 of Paul's letter to the Romans: 'Love in all sincerity, loathing evil and clinging to the good. Let love for our brotherhood breed warmth of mutual affection. Give pride of place to one another in esteem

. . . with unflagging energy, in ardour of spirit, serve the Lord. Let hope keep you joyful; in trouble stand firm; persist in prayer.'

Easier said than done. Hard enough to be a Christian at any time, harder still to be both a Christian and an active, committed police officer. Dice saw so much of pain and suffering, of the baser side of humankind. The public come to the police only in times of stress, when they are anguished or angry or empty-hearted from loss, showing themselves distorted by emotion.

Dice tried to pray but he felt no contact and the words would not come. He felt desperately weary, tired in body and spirit. He slept for a while.

His dreams were confused and fragmented, centred on scenes of dark hopelessness. In many his wife appeared, sometimes as victim, sometimes as a figure of evil. Equally often Paul Carpenter appeared, but Carpenter was always the victim and Dice the concerned but powerless onlooker. Always Paul Carpenter died, and then Dice was alone, totally alone in an enveloping blackness, cold of heart and desperately alone.

When he woke the aspirin had dulled the pain in his head. He got up and went back into the control room. Jean Peck searched his face with worried eyes.

'Are you all right, Dice?'

'I'm fine. Just a headache. Anything happening?'

'They're bedded down for the night, sir,' said Corelli.

'Remind me in the morning to tell Colin Land they're armed with Kalashnikov automatic rifles.'

'I thought he knew.'

'No. I forgot to tell him.'

'But he's seen the monitor tapes, part of them.'

He may have missed it.'

Corelli shrugged.

'It doesn't mean a lot. They're two a penny anywhere round the Middle East.'

'I know.'

'My turn to stay the night,' said Corelli pointedly.

'Yes. Make sure you get some sleep.'

'I will.'

Dice made no move to go. Corelli looked at his watch.

'It's gone eleven.'

'Go home, Dice. You'll be no bloody good to anyone without proper rest,' said Tickner, 'doctor's orders.'

'He's right, Dice,' said Jean Peck. But it was said reluctantly.

'I know when I'm not wanted,' Dice said.

He bid them all goodnight and walked down to the pavement, past the wooden hoardings garishly lit by the floodlights. Behind the command van at the end of Spencer Road were the massed ranks of the media, cameras, technicians, reporters.

His arrival raised a ripple of interest but he kept well away from them, got into his car and was driven quickly away.

There were no lights on in his house. He let himself in, went to the kitchen and made himself a cup of coffee. The silence, the loneliness depressed him.

He went upstairs and got ready for bed. He remained awake until 1 a.m. trying to read a book, then he fell asleep.

His wife had still not returned.

THURSDAY

33 At 2 a.m. the girl terrorist spoke to her partner.

'It's time,' she whispered.

He was instantly awake.

She went to the kitchen area, took a broom from a cupboard and handed it to him.

'Hook it in,' she said.

She held back the curtains and slid the french windows open. He lay flat on the floor and pulled the landline receiver towards him with the broom.

When it was inside the room the girl closed the french windows, let the curtain drop back into place and picked up the receiver. The voice answered almost instantly and she was aware of a faint stirring of suspicion, but she had geared herself to the moment and that warning was lost in the ensuing conversation.

'Chief Superintendent Corelli,' said the voice.

'Get Dice,' said the girl.

'He's not here at the moment, I can get him to the phone in half an hour. In the meantime, I'm his second-in-command, you can talk to me . . .'

'No.'

'Very well, I'll call Mr Dice.'

Corelli's voice was quiet, reassuring, almost placatory.

'Do that. Give him a message,' the girl ordered.

'Yes?'

'Tell him if he wants the hostages alive we want an escort to Hendon aerodrome and a fuelled-up executive jet waiting for us there at ten this morning.

'I don't think . . .' Corelli began gently.

'Ten a.m. is the deadline. Just tell him,' said the girl, and slammed down the receiver.

The man smiled at her. She took up her blanket and went to an armchair.

'Your watch,' she said, out loud.

The hostages were awake. The girl's eyes were wide with apprehension, Carpenter's alert and calculating.

After a while it seemed that the girl terrorist had gone to sleep.

34 Corelli had been woken the moment the male terrorist had taken the broom from the cupboard, and he telephoned Dice as the landline was drawn into the siege flat.

The insistent ringing of the telephone pulled Dice unwillingly from his bed. As he got up and switched on the bedside lamp he saw that he was still alone in the room. The fact registered with him, inflicted momentary pain, then he put it from his mind. He went downstairs into the hall, picked up the phone. He knew it would be Corelli.

'Yes, Ray?' he said.

Corelli explained.

'Have you woken Tickner and Peck?'

'Yes, as soon as we saw what was happening. What about the Commissioner, sir?'

'Wait. You said the girl has gone to sleep?'

'She seems to have, sir.'

Dice was waiting outside his home when the car slid quietly in to the kerb. He felt light-headed from his sudden awakening, his eyes prickled as if he had grit on his eyeballs, his mouth felt dry, he found it hard to concentrate.

As the car sped him across London through empty streets he struggled with the information Corelli had given him. He considered it not to be chance that the terrorists had chosen this hour to make contact. Then, the girl had apparently gone to sleep. Since she did not know she was under visual observation she had not done it for effect, it was genuine coolness, unconcern. And that bothered him greatly.

He found Corelli, Tickner and Peck hunched forward in their seats, hugging cups of coffee in their hands, staring at the monitor. Corelli was dressed but the two doctors wore dressing gowns over their nightclothes. Tickner looked tousled and sleepy but Jean Peck had put on a face.

There was no action on the monitor. Dice threw his coat on to a chairback and greeted them.

'Anything else happened?' he asked.

'No, sir. It's been just as you see it. You know, I'm beginning to think they've been through this before.'

'Or something like it,' said Dice. 'The arrangement was I would contact them when I arrive?'

'Yes.'

Dice picked up the landline receiver and depressed the call button, watching the monitor as he did so. He saw the man get up and shake the girl's shoulder. She did not hurry, taking time to come fully awake. Then she went to the kitchen area, splashed water on her face from a bucket and dried herself before picking up the telephone. Dice almost spoke, remembering only just in time to let her speak first.

'Yeah?' said the girl.

'This is Commander Dice.'

There was a fractional hesitation before the girl spoke again.

'You know what we want?' she asked.

'I've been told.'

'You've got the deadline. I've given you plenty of time, there'll be no extensions. At ten a.m. we shoot Carpenter and throw him over the balcony.'

'And then what?' asked Dice.

'What?'

'After you kill Carpenter.'

'Don't get funny with me, Dice.'

'I'm serious. After Carpenter you give us another deadline. Then, when we don't keep it, you kill the girl. Then you have no hostages, we come in and get you.'

'You can't take that line, Dice. Your job's to see they stay alive.'

'We both have cards. It's just a matter of how we play them.'

'We kill Carpenter then come out shooting with the girl in front, that's how I play. You want that?'

The girl's voice had risen slightly but she still had herself under tight control.

'We can't give you an aeroplane,' said Dice mildly. 'You know that. But we can talk another deal.'

'No deals.'

'I'd like to speak to the hostages, be sure they're alive and well, then I'll send in food, a toilet . . .'

'Forget it, Dice. Just do as I say or Carpenter dies,' and the girl slammed down the receiver.

Dice stood, receiver in hand, watching the monitor. The terrorists were standing close together, whispering. Then the girl returned to her armchair and covered herself with the blanket. The man looked as if he wanted to talk further but after watching her for a moment, he too returned to his armchair, cuddling his Kalashnikov automatic rifle to his chest.

'What do you think, Jean?' Dice asked, replacing the landline receiver.

'They are remarkably controlled,' she said.

'Yes, but will they kill him?'

'Only if it's expedient, I think. Only if it serves a purpose, not from anger or spite or . . . but that's right at this moment, things could change.'

'But at this moment?'

Jean Peck bit her lip in concentration, aware of the heavy responsibility upon her, aware that if Dice accepted her evaluation and she were wrong, the death of the hostages would be a burden she would carry to the grave.

'They came here intending to execute both Pope and Carpenter,' Dice added.

'You think so, they intend to kill Carpenter anyway?'

'Yes, I'm sure of it.'

Jean shook her head.

'Then why ask me?'

'I want to know if they will kill him now, in the next few hours, at the deadline.'

Jean Peck said nothing.

'The decision is mine,' said Dice gently, 'whatever you say, in the end I take full responsibility.'

And somehow that made Jean Peck's decision all the harder.

'I don't think they'll kill him yet,' she said finally.

'Thank you, Jean.'

'When you talk to them next,' Tickner put in, 'if you talk a deal, include getting the hostages ungagged and unbound.'

'We don't know they *are* gagged and bound, Bob,' said Dice.

'Eh?'

'We can't let them know we have a window into that room, it might provoke them into some precipitate action.'

'Damn! I'd forgotten.'

'I'll do what I can.'

Then Dice telephoned the Commissioner at his home. Sir John Cowling answered surprisingly quickly. Dice brought him up to date.

'I'll come down,' said Sir John.

'There's no hurry, sir. The deadline's not until ten a.m.'

'Will they do it, kill Carpenter? What does the psychiatrist say?'

'She and I are in agreement. They won't kill him over this deadline.'

'What makes you think that?'

'They don't know we have a camera in there. What they are saying does not square with what we see they are doing.'

'But they've still left you with an ultimatum.'

'Yes. But the next move is up to me. I think we shall be able to talk a deal to make things easier for the hostages. I don't think we will have to face the deadline.'

'I hope you're right, Allan.'

'So do I, sir.'

At 4.30 a.m. the terrorists changed guard. They held a whispered conference in which the man seemed to be impressing something on the girl. After a moment she cut him short with an abrupt gesture and he slammed himself angrily into an armchair.

'Trouble in the camp?' said Corelli hopefully.

'She's the boss, Dice. He's the weak link,' said the psychiatrist.

'She's strong enough for both of them,' said Dice, 'and if he steps too far out of line she'll kill him.'

The others stared at him.

'You really think so?' said Doctor Tickner, doubtfully.

'Dice is right,' said Jean Peck.

'It's a matter of discipline,' said Dice. 'Absolute discipline is essential for their survival.'

He waited until 5 a.m. before using the landline again. When the call bell sounded, the man was instantly awake, if in fact he had been asleep. The girl inclined her thumb and it was the man who answered.

'Yeah?'

'This is Dice.'

'So?'

'Would you like me to send in a portable toilet, some food?'

The man said nothing for a moment but on the monitor the watchers saw him look across to the girl. She nodded. He turned back to the receiver, his body movements suggesting an eagerness that his words belied.

'If you like, but the deadline stays.'

'We can talk about that later. For now, let me speak to the hostages and in return I'll send in the food.'

Silence again. But the man pointed at the hostages, made a talking mime with his fingers and looked enquiringly at the girl. Again she nodded.

'And the toilet?'

'Yes.'

'They're okay, alive and well.'

'The deal is, I talk to them first.'

The girl had got up and was removing the gags from the hostages' mouths.

'Wait,' said the man.

He picked up the landline receiver and pulled the trailing cord across to the hostages, holding the mouthpiece out to Carpenter.

'This is the police,' the man said to Carpenter, 'tell them you're okay, watch what you say.'

'Hullo?' said Carpenter, his voice dry and croaked.

'This is Commander Dice, Reverend Carpenter?'

'Yes.'

'Are you physically well?'

'Yes, but we're bound and gagged, can you persuade them at least to release my secretary?'

Dice could have wept with joy. Carpenter had given him exactly what he wanted.

'I'll do what I can,' he said.

The man snatched away the mouthpiece.

'Satisfied, Dice?' he said.

'The girl,' said Dice, 'I'd like to speak to the girl.'

At first Mary Tü was unable to articulate.

'Talk to him!' shouted the man.

'Hullo,' Mary Tü said, fearfully.

'Just try to relax, Miss Tü,' said Dice. 'Are you reasonably well?'

The man snatched the mouthpiece away before she could answer.

'You heard her, she's okay. Now send the stuff in. None of that hot soup business, proper food, we want meat, bread and butter, salad, fruit . . . and some beer and cigarettes. And don't forget the toilet.'

'The deal was food, not a banquet.'

'Now you listen . . .'

'You can have it, everything you've asked for,' said Dice quickly, 'but in return untie the hostages and leave them free, don't gag them again, they can't do you any harm, can they?'

Again, on the monitor, they saw the man translate in mime and the girl's nod.

'Okay,' said the man.

'It will take half an hour to collect the food. We'll lower it down on to the balcony. One last thing . . .'

'Yeah?'

'You might consider releasing Miss Tü, she's . . .'

'Stuff it, Dice. And just remember not to drop anything in the food by mistake. They eat first and if they drop off to sleep suddenly you've got problems, I promise you.'

And he slammed down the receiver.

Dice replaced his receiver but continued to watch the monitor. The man was grinning. He gave the thumbs-up sign to the girl. She smiled briefly in return, then relaxed into the armchair. Neither of them bothered to replace the hostages' gags.

'Well done, sir,' said Corelli.

'I didn't do anything,' said Dice, 'they did.'

'Why did the man answer this time?' asked Dr Tickner.

'They've reversed the age-old interrogation technique,' said Corelli. 'You know, one is the hard man, one the father figure? She let him take over so they could make the deal.'

'Which means she wanted the deal as much as he did,' said Jean.

'And she doesn't lose face,' said Tickner.

'She's not concerned about face,' said Dice.

'What, then?'

'By using him to negotiate she gets what she wants but at any time she can step in and change the scenario.'

'She's no fool,' said Jean, 'she's operating a psychological battle against us.'

'Since you two're inside her mind,' said Tickner, 'what does she really want?'

'She wants an aircraft,' said Corelli.

'She wants to keep the initiative,' said Dice.

35 The Commissioner arrived at 5.30 a.m., just as the food and portable toilet were being lowered into the balcony of the siege flat. He motioned the others to resume their seats and took a chair to join them in watching the monitor.

Paul Carpenter was pushed out on to the balcony to collect the packages. He seemed to have difficulty in bending over to pick them up.

'Stiff as a pole, poor blighter,' commented Dr Tickner.

Inside the room, the terrorists fed samples of the food and drink to the hostages, then set up the portable toilet in a corner and made use of it in turn. Then they permitted the hostages to do the same. They seemed in no hurry to take food themselves. The man emptied the cigarettes out of the packets on to a table, then selected some at random and split them open. Only then did he take one and light it up. The girl did the same.

'Careful, aren't they?' said Sir John.

'Efficient, sir,' said Dice. 'Everything they do is calculated and efficient.'

He ran back the television tape of the night's events for the benefit of the Commissioner together with the limited information the bugging equipment had collected.

Then Sir John spoke privately with Dice in the spartan bedroom.

'They obviously know we've got the room under audio surveillance,' Sir John commented.

'Yes,' said Dice.

'And we still have this deadline.'

'At the moment.'

'I have an appointment with the Home Secretary at ten-thirty, should I cancel it?'

'No need, sir. If you'll be in your office just after ten, if you can delay leaving for that long, I'll telephone you immediately the deadline has passed.'

'You seem confident they won't kill Carpenter.'

'They won't kill him on this deadline.'

'Killing Carpenter was one of the reasons they came here. Wouldn't the deadline be as good a time as any? They might think that by a show of force they could persuade us to give them an aircraft. They'd still have the girl as hostage.'

'That is logical reasoning, sir. But they don't really want an aircraft, they know we would never provide one. They have something else in mind.'

'What?'

'I don't know yet.'

'Allan, you do understand that for many reasons we cannot afford to be wrong about this?'

'Yes.'

'All human life may be equal in the eyes of the Lord, Allan, but the hard fact is that some human lives are more equal than others. We must get Carpenter out of this alive. That is more important than the arrest of the terrorists.'

'We're not likely to get one without the other, sir. As you said, they came here to execute him.'

'Don't get me wrong, Allan. I want them, I'm just saying that if, because of the changed situation they're in, it comes to one or the other, we take Carpenter.'

'And the girl?'

'His secretary? Yes, of course, her as well.'

'But her life is not of the same order of priority.'

'Don't be difficult, Allan.'

'Our first priority has always been, as a matter of policy, the preservation of the lives of the hostages, all hostages regardless of who they are. I want to understand, in this case has that policy changed, am I to deal with the terrorists on the basis of their freedom for Carpenter's life?'

'No. We cannot do that. It doesn't work, only encourages another attempt or they take him along and kill him out of our airspace. Hell, man! You know that!'

'Exactly. I just wanted to be sure in view of what you said, sir.'

'I said just this: if, in the end, we're up against a blank wall, if the time comes when you are sure that if you don't give something they will kill him, then you must give to save his life. That is not a suggestion contrary to established policy.'

'No, sir. Just a shift in emphasis.'

'Quite.'

'Which is fine so long as the terrorists get no inkling of it.'

'That's your job, Mr Dice.'

The formal use of his name was clear indication to Dice that he had trod as far as he could in this particular minefield.

'I shall be in my office,' said Sir John.

'Very well, sir.'

'I shall not be able to attend the morning conference here but I shall want a verbal report from you at . . . say 2 p.m.'

'Of course, sir.'

'And Allan . . .'

'Sir?'

'You are obviously tired. I know it's difficult, but try to snatch the odd hour's rest.'

'I'll try, sir.'

When the Commissioner had left, Corelli sidled up to Dice.

'What did he say, sir?' he asked.

'He told me to rest,' said Dice.

And he walked through to his makeshift bedroom and closed the door.

36

CODE: EAD. 5.J. FROM KARELIN EX LONDON REFERENTURA TO DIAKENOV EXECUTIVE ACTION DEPT. 1ST CHIEF

DIRECTORATE. ON ARRIVAL POPE DEAD CARPENTER HOSTAGE. AGENTS IN SIEGE. CONTACT IMPOSSIBLE. INSTRUCTIONS. END.

37 At 9.57 a.m., three minutes to the deadline, Dice picked up the landline receiver and depressed the call button.

There were seven people in the room, all eyes on the monitor screen, all ears strained to hear what Dice was to say. The atmosphere was heavy with apprehension, brittle with tension.

Only Dice seemed relaxed and unconcerned as he waited patiently for the terrorists to react. The man answered.

'Yeah?'

'This is Dice.'

'So?'

The man put his hand over the mouthpiece and beckoned to the girl. She stood beside him and he inclined the receiver so she could hear. Dice watched them, did not speak until the girl was in position.

'The food was acceptable?' he asked.

'Yes.'

'You have untied the hostages?'

'Just like I said.'

Dice knew this for the truth. The hostages had been untied an hour after the food had been delivered. They were at that moment sitting on the floor, watching the terrorists, listening to one side of the conversation.

'Fine,' said Dice.

'What the hell do you want, Dice?' asked the man.

Dice wanted just one thing, to keep them talking until the deadline had passed, to remove the pressure on them to take some action at the stated time. He looked at his watch. It was one minute to ten.

'I'd like to speak to Carpenter.'

'Balls.'

'I kept my word. I just want to ask him if he's free, as you promised.'

'I told you.'

'Forgive me . . . it will only take a moment.'

On the monitor screen they saw the man look questioningly at the girl. She was clearly undecided. Then she shrugged and walked across to where Carpenter and Mary Tü were sitting together on the floor.

'Ask him if he's untied, that's all,' said the man.

'Very well.'

The girl whispered emphatically into Carpenter's ear then pulled him to his feet, leading him to the telephone.

Dice looked at his watch. It was 10 a.m. Corelli gave the thumbs-up sign. There were smiles of relief in the command room.

'Here he is,' said the man.

'Reverend Carpenter?' said Dice.

'Yes, is that Mr Dice?'

'It is. Have you and Miss Tü been untied?'

'Yes, we have . . .'

'No gags?'

'No. Thank you, Mr Dice, God bless you and guide you in what you have to do . . .'

The man snatched the phone away.

'Enough of the crap. Dice . . .?'

'Yes.'

'You heard him.'

'Yes, thank you.'

'We want that plane.'

'I know.'

'What about it?'

'I'm sure you know I have a problem there.'

'Solve it.'

'I cannot provide an aircraft for you.'

'Then find someone who can.'

'There *is* no one who can. A political decision was made long ago not to permit such a thing. I can help in other ways though.'

'A fair trial, all that juice?'

'It matters. There are many places in the world where you would not get a fair trial.'

'There's not going to be a trial. Just get that plane.'

The man put down the receiver. But the deadline was past and the terrorists had not set another.

Dice telephoned the Commissioner.

38 Firth entered a public telephone box near Parliament Square. After a few moments the telephone rang.

'Firth,' he said, as if he were in his own office.

'I have something for you,' Maztikyan said.

'Yes, Leonid?'

'Karelin arrived yesterday.'

'Why didn't you tell me when we met?'

'I did not know why he was here then.'

'Who is he to kill?'

'The terrorists.'

'He's a little late, I fear.'

'Yes. He was sent before we knew about the siege.'

'And now?'

'He has reported back, he's waiting for instructions.'

'Why do your people want them?'

Maztikyan told him.

'So, very embarrassing for you.'

'Yes. You must make me a promise.'

'If I can.'

'Use this information, but not openly. It could only have come from inside the Referentura, you understand?'

'Of course.'

'I have your word?'

'You have, Leonid. And when Karelin gets his reply, you'll let me know what it is?'

'Yes.'

'Fine.'

'Roger?'

'Yes.'

'What did that girl do with the candles?'

39 The conference took place at 2.30 p.m. in the lounge of the ground-floor flat of the house that Dice had commandeered as a forward command post.

Deputy Assistant Commissioner (Ops) Ben Yallop was present but he conceded the chairmanship to Dice, declaring himself as an observer. Apart from Dice and Corelli, present were Commander Land, Special Branch, Commander Peach, Fingerprints, Commander Delabole, Criminal Intelligence and Technical Support, and Detective Inspector Beal of Dice's Anti-Terrorist Squad whose function was to take minutes from the tape of the meeting.

Dice brought them up to date, then went round the table taking reports from each of the department heads. He gave first opportunity to Commander Peach.

'Anything for us, Stan?'

'Plenty. I can tie in those two,' he pointed vaguely in the direction of the siege flat, 'with both the vehicles, and with marks found on the door of Pope's flat.'

'But can you identify them?'

'No. No trace of fingerprint records here nor in the half-dozen other forces that've so far replied. I think you can take it they've no form in this country.'

Dice was not surprised. He turned to Commander Delabole.

'Mike?'

'No trace by photograph in criminal intelligence records, I'm afraid. Of course, if you had names, we might be able to help rather more. I think we're rather wasting our time to be honest, old chap, they're visitors, probably never been here before.'

'You may be right, Mike,' said Dice. And then, to Commander Land, 'which leaves you as our best hope, Colin.'

'I can tell you Dice, we don't know these people. They have never come to notice before. I agree with Mike, they've been imported to do the job.'

'Colin, this thing is international news, *someone* must be talking.'

'Everybody's talking, no one's saying anything.'

'You said you could make a guess as to what group they represent.'

'I've a meeting arranged for tonight. I'll phone you after. I can't promise anything.'

'Gentlemen, I'm working in the dark,' Dice said. 'I don't know who these people are, who is backing them, what motivates them. Without that information I have to concede them the initiative . . . and that is potentially disastrous.'

'You'll have to string them along until we can get something for you,' said Land.

'The trouble is, Dice, old friend,' said Delabole, 'the field's wide open. Read the papers, listen to the news reporters, everyone has his or her own theory as to who's behind it.'

'And we're in the same boat,' Peach put in.

Land took over the argument.

'Every branch of international and internal politics has its lunatic fringe,' he said. 'We dare not concentrate our efforts on the political left. The Christian Democrat Party don't have many friends. They're a threat to all the other political parties, to the establishment as a whole, even the Church is sitting on the fence. About the only thing the Communists and the Fascists agree on is that the Christian Democrats are bad news.'

'The people don't think so,' Dice said.

'Sod the people!' said Land. 'We're talking about who might have sent in this execution squad. I'm telling you it could be just about anybody.'

'I think we should be able to narrow the field,' said Dice.

'You're being pig-headed, Dice, old chap,' said Delabole. 'These Christian Democrat bods are advocating revolution, d'you realize that? What with their decentralization of political power, ruralization policies, proportional representation, bill of rights, individual worker contracts, self-sufficiency tax grants and God alone knows what else . . . nothing will ever be the same again if they get power.'

'Which might be no bad thing,' said Dice.

'That's not the point,' said Peach. 'Consider this, they've got an answer for every social and political problem, or so they say, but every one of their ideas has been pinched from the other political ideologies. They've just lumped them together, then larded the lot with the implicit suggestion that God is on their side. No one likes having his ideas pinched. But they've not only upset the other political groups, they've upset the unions, the bosses, the Civil Service, even the Church is split.'

'Who has ever given up power willingly?' said Dice. 'Even so, of all the power groups the Christian Democrats have upset, very few would have either the desire or the capability to send in an execution squad.'

'I give up,' said Peach.

'Don't do that,' said Dice, permitting a rare smile.

'Let me put something else to you, Dice,' said Land. 'If I wanted to carry out an execution in Russia I wouldn't send an Englishman. I'd pick and train someone who was fanatically anti-communist, someone who was a Russian *émigré* or at least half-Russian and I'd arm him or her with Chinese weapons. I know that, you know that, so do the Russians and the Chinese. It's simple. Everyone knows what you have to do, therefore the fact that this pair you've got holed up speak perfect English with an American accent and are armed with Russian weapons means nothing, tells us nothing about them or who set them up. Now if they were black as the ace of spades, armed with bows and arrows and only spoke Swahili we might be able to narrow things down. As it is, we need time.'

'We don't *have* time,' said Dice, 'but I know you are all doing your best. No one could ask for more.'

'Except the Reverend Dice,' said Delabole laconically.

'Ask and ye shall receive,' Dice said blandly.

'But not from us, we're only mortals,' said Land.

The meeting broke up. Dice was acutely depressed. It had served no purpose, no gains had been made.

Deputy Assistant Commissioner Yallop had taken no part in the meeting but when all the others had left the room he spoke to Dice.

'Can you turn your mind to something else for a moment, Dice?' he asked.

'Just about, sir.'

'I must advise you to watch your back.'

'Why?'

'Not why, who.'

'I'm sorry, sir. I don't understand.'

'You're a good policeman, Dice, but you have a way of upsetting people. You're too independent, that's not always appreciated in a hierarchical institution. And you let your religious beliefs show, that makes people uncomfortable . . . and worst of all you won't involve yourself in the internal politics of the force, and that makes people suspicious.'

'I'm a detective, not a public relations expert.'

'You see? Listen, Dice, strictly between you and me, watch out for Mr Cottar . . . he's after your head.'

'Why should the A.C.C. want my head?'

'I've given you the reasons. Add the fact that you get too much publicity, you have too much publicly known success. What king would accept being outshone by one of his courtiers?'

'King?'

'Mr Cottar has his ambitions.'

'I see. And you, sir, you have ambitions?'

'Naturally.'

'I see.'

'However, that need not concern you. I like an easy life. A few brilliant courtiers would ensure that for me. You understand?'

'Perfectly.'

'Now get on with the job, forget what I've said. You can rely on my support.'

'I hope I don't need it, sir,' said Dice.

And he left the room.

Yallop smiled at the closed door. Dice was not the most eager of recruits. Perhaps it did not matter overmuch. In the end the truly independent man can be relied upon as much as the overtly committed ally.

40

Commander Land telephoned the control room at 8 p.m. and asked to speak to Dice.

'I'll be along to see you in about half an hour,' he said.

'You have something for me?' Dice asked.

'Something. Not very much. It may help.'

Dice repeated the conversation to Corelli.

'It must be good. He'd never say a word unless he were sure,' Corelli said.

Doctor Tickner was taking a meal but Jean Peck was in the room.

'Can he identify them, Dice?' she asked.

'Perhaps.'

'Be nice to know our enemy. I'm getting square eyes.'

'They'd be beautiful any shape,' said Dice, but he was not looking at her, his mind was clearly elsewhere.

'Can I have a word, sir?' Corelli said.

He led the way into the spartan bedroom.

'What is it, Ray?' Dice enquired.

'My wife's gone to stay with her mother.'

'Oh?'

'She thought it best whilst this job's on. Taken the children and so forth.'

'No trouble?' said Dice anxiously.

'Of course not, you know Peggy, takes it as it comes. Anyway, saves me a visit from mother-in-law. Best all round, I can bed down here.'

'Every night?'

'Why not? Suits me.'

'Very well, Ray. I have no objections, so long as you're sure.'

I'm sure. It means you can go home nights.'

'I do well enough.'

'You missed out last night. It makes sense. Why hang about here when there's no need. You know I'd call you instantly if anything looked like boiling up.'

'We'll see.'

'That's settled then. Couple of other things. The forensic reports on both vehicles and the Yard bomb have arrived, they're down in the command van. I didn't bother to bring them up because they're not very informative. Useful stuff if we get into court but no help at the moment. The only thing is, the bomb was a sophisticated type of P.E. made in France. There's also a lot of guff from the press release of the photofit pictures. Our boys are running around like mad dogs but it's all rubbish so far. That's it.'

'They had to stay somewhere, we'll find the place.'

'Talking of domiciles, how is it Carpenter can afford an expensive flat in Hampstead?' Corelli asked.

'It was left to the Party by a wealthy patron a few years back. It doesn't belong to him.'

'They seem to have plenty of money, the Christian Democrats, where does it all come from?'

'Private contributions, fund raising, wills. People treat the Party as a kind of charity or like giving money to the Church. They consider they are investing in their own future, so they are generous.'

'Even so, it's painful parting with cash. Even to the Church.'

'It always seems odd to me, Ray. You go to church now and again, but you apparently don't believe in God.'

'Oh I do. More or less. It's the done thing in my family, going to church. I suppose I see it as a kind of insurance, just in case he *is* up there.'

'But you doubt it.'

'I just don't know. You could say I believe in going to church but I don't think you should make a religion of it.'

'You could try,' said Dice.

Colin Land arrived just before nine o'clock.

'I'd like us to talk alone,' he said.

'Would you mind if Corelli were present?'

'Er . . . no.'

They went through into the bedroom. It was now so often used as an adjunct to the control room that Dice had had chairs and a table brought in.

'What is it, Colin?' Dice asked.

'How much do you know about the International Workers Brotherhood?'

'Not a great deal. Just another Communist front organization.'

'That's right. They've been going a long time, actually the organization was set up in 1948 but it was allowed to remain dormant until 1963. It had four years of activity then went dormant again until eighteen months ago.'

'Are you saying the I.W.B. is behind this?'

'Not exactly, it's a little more complicated than that. The I.W.B. was originally formed after the Second World War as a back-up organization in case the communist-controlled World Federation of Trade Unions failed to capture the support of union leaders in the capitalist countries. In the event, that support was not needed and in 1963 the K.G.B. took over the organization, lock, stock and barrel.'

'What did they want it for?'

'Probably to act as a bank, a clearing house for paying foreign agents, supplying equipment, training terrorists and so on. It has the benefit that the I.W.B. headquarters is in Djakarta, well away from home.'

'Then what we have here is a K.G.B. operation.'

'I don't think so. In 1970 the K.G.B. was getting a bad press internationally. You remember we aimed 107 agents out of this country alone, and they withdrew their horns a little. One of the things they did was to hand over control of the I.W.B. to some trusted stooges. Exactly what has happened since then I'm not sure, I may be able to find out later.'

'It's not like the K.G.B. to hand over complete control of

anything, they must at least have had agents in the organization.'

'I'm sure that's true but I think what may have happened is that the I.W.B., once it was free of direct K.G.B. control, was infiltrated by people who were far more radical than the present Russian Communist Party. These people wanted action, and were not prepared to bide their time waiting for the K.G.B. to put them to use.'

'You think the K.G.B. bred a monster they can't control?'

'It could be that way.'

'I can't believe the K.G.B. would allow that to happen,' Corelli put it. 'The head of the K.G.B. is also a member of the Politburo. To have K.G.B. trained and financed terrorists acting on their own initiative could have disastrous political implications for the Russians.'

'Quite so,' said Land. 'I think they have tried. The last International Conference of the I.W.B. was held in Djakarta a year ago. At that meeting a man named Elias Pina was elected General Secretary. Let me recall two incidents that have occurred in the last year: you remember the murder of Bishop Mtali in Cape Town?'

'Yes, of course.'

'And Senator McNaught in Detroit?'

'Yes. You think Pina was responsible?'

'It seems likely that he was. Another point, both men were leading political campaigns with a strong religious element.'

'And the K.G.B. have done nothing about Pina?'

'I think that initially they found themselves in some difficulty. How could they be seen to eliminate socialist freedom fighters? Think what capital the Chinese would make out of that. In the event, it looks as if they did put pressure on Pina. The headquarters in Djakarta were closed down about three months ago and they moved to Zurich. I think it was a compromise, no doubt the K.G.B. would have preferred to have had him behind the curtain where they could control him.'

'Is it possible that Pina is in fact a Chinese agent?'

'Unlikely. He was trained by the Russians, in Cuba I believe. He may have been turned since then, of course. In any event his career is over now.'

'How come?'

'Two days ago the headquarters of the I.W.B. in Zurich was closed down. Pina is now a guest of the K.G.B. at Dzerzhinsky Square.'

'Poor old Pina,' said Corelli.

'Exactly.'

'We don't know the names of these two?' Dice asked, pointing across the road.

'No. I may find out.'

'It would help. Anyway, you've given me almost everything I need. When I tell them that their organization is dead, Pina inside, they'll be more likely to listen to reason. They can expect no help now.'

'I'm afraid you can't repeat anything I've said outside this room, not even to the terrorists.'

Dice stared at him in disbelief.

'Why ever not?'

'This information came from non-police sources, you understand?'

'Yes.'

'I'm told that my friend had no trouble at all in discovering this information. No difficulties were placed in his way. That suggests the K.G.B. had no real objections to our knowing.'

'I can understand that. For once we share an interest.'

'Perhaps.'

'You said yourself you didn't think the K.G.B. were involved, surely this proves it.'

'That is my belief but my contact makes another point. Nothing is simple in the world of espionage. This in fact might still be a K.G.B. operation, a complicated set-up to achieve their object, and provide themselves with a ready-made alibi to the world. We can't afford to take that chance.'

'The press in this country have already speculated that this is a K.G.B. operation. They read our papers, they must know by now that if that was the object it has failed. Anyway, these terrorists are going nowhere but jail for a long time. What difference does it make what I say to them over the landline?'

'It can't be done, Dice.'

'It has to be done, Colin. We can go right to the top to make sure it is.'

Land stood.

'I came here straight from a meeting in Whitehall with the Commissioner, the Home Secretary and the Prime Minister. The answer is no. Use what I've told you as best you can but not directly, those are the instructions, Dice.'

Dice was on his feet now, uncharacteristically angry.

'It makes no damn sense, Colin . . .'

'It makes a hell of a lot of sense, Dice. Where d'you think this information came from?'

'Obviously you have a contact in the Security Services . . .'

'Exactly. And his information came from inside the Russian Embassy. What we don't know is whether his agent has genuinely turned or whether he's talking because the K.G.B. have told him to. We don't know if we've got the truth or just what the K.G.B. want us to believe. Either way that agent *has* to be protected. He's a big noise, he might prove invaluable. This job of yours is only a drop in the ocean compared to what he might give in the future, *if* he's genuine. You understand now?'

Dice sat on the edge of the bed.

'I understand quite well,' he said.

Land was at the door, ready to leave.

'I'm sorry, Dice. That's the way it is, but you're better armed now than before I came. I'll be in touch.'

Corelli saw him out. Dice went into the control room, stood staring at the monitor screen. Jean Peck screwed round in her chair to look at him.

'Anything?' she asked.

'You can work on the assumption that those two are

ideologically motivated,' said Dice, 'that they have been well trained, well prepared mentally and physically for just such an eventuality as this siege.'

'Dice, I could have told *you* that. Is that all?'

'I'm afraid so.'

Corelli came back into the room. He and Dice sat down to watch the monitor. The hostages were sitting together on the floor, the terrorists at a table playing cards.

'When I was in the army,' Corelli began, 'I was put on guard duty, guarding the motor transport lines . . .'

Dice looked at him. Encouraged, Corelli continued.

'. . . They took away my rifle. I asked the Sergeant why, if the trucks were so important they required a guard, I had been deprived of the means to best do the job.'

Dice smiled a little, Corelli always had a fund of apt stories.

'And what did the Sergeant say?' he asked.

'Not very much. He called it "conduct prejudicial to good order and military discipline", something like that. I did four days in the pokey.'

'That's life for you,' said Dice.

'The point is, he let me do the guard duty before he put me on the fizzer. The camp wasn't fenced and a local yobbo ran out of petrol for his motorbike, wandered into the M.T. lines and began siphoning petrol from one of the trucks. If I'd had the rifle it would've been easy but when he saw that I wasn't armed, he had a go at me with a knife. A nasty piece of work that young man.'

'And . . .?'

Corelli shrugged and grinned.

'Rifle or no rifle, the result was the same in the end. I kicked him in the crotch.'

41 At 11 p.m. the terrorists fed their captives, permitted them to use the toilet, then settled down for the night. The officers attending the surveillance equipment were relieved by the night duty men and the two doctors arranged shifts between themselves.

Dice left at 11.30 p.m. and went home. His driver deposited him outside the house and Dice was a little surprised to see it ablaze with light.

Betty was in the living room, sprawled on a settee, the floor littered with records and record covers. The record player was silent, she was selecting from L.P.s in a heap on her lap. Beside her, on the arm of the settee, was an ashtray overflowing with butt-ends and a glass of neat vodka.

'Want a drink, Dice?' she asked.

'Yes, I will.'

She got up and poured it for him. He made to kiss her as she brought it to him. She seemed surprised, caught off balance. She leant him a cheek, then moved away, switched off the record player.

'I won't put any more on. We'll drink this and go up, eh?'

'As you wish.'

'How's it going?' she asked.

But she was not really interested.

'We've made some progress.'

'Oh.'

'I came home last night, but I was called out again.'

'What time?'

'Two in the morning.'

'Stinking job.'

No mention of why she had not been there. No apology. And from Dice, no questions, no recriminations.

'You've not been out today?'

'No. Did some housework, got some food in.'

She yawned, finished off her drink at a gulp.

'Take me to bed, Dice,' she said.

There was nothing seductive in the invitation. It was an expression of hunger, of need.

She was undressed before him, in the bed and waiting, irritated at his slowness.

'Come *on*, Dice!'

Her hands fluttered over his body, she rubbed her breasts against him, constantly in movement. But he remained unmoved, incapable of responding.

He knew he was being used. He knew the act she required of him was simple animal lust. Love had no part in it. Her need was entirely physical and that knowledge robbed him of his virility.

'What the *hell's* the matter, Dice?'

'Perhaps I'm tired.'

She pushed herself away from him.

' "Perhaps I'm tired",' she mimicked ferociously. 'Perhaps you're just not bloody well up to it!'

He knew he should try. It was his duty. Also, he loved her, God help him. But when she was like this, so bluntly and coldly demanding, he could do nothing. Her very need emasculated him.

Then her need overcame her anger. She took his hand and placed it in position.

'At least do that, Dice. Do *something* for me.'

But he felt only revulsion. He took away his hand. He could do nothing for her, nothing at all.

She flung herself out of the bed, her naked body taut with anger and frustration.

'I'm sorry . . .' he said.

'You're always sorry.'

'It wasn't always like this.'

'No. You could perform once. These last six months, nothing. You're useless, Dice.'

It was a bitterly unfair attack, but, as always, he accepted the blame. He looked away from her.

'If I left it to you I'd never get any, would I?'

She was standing there hating him, trying to hurt him.

'You should've been a bloody monk, Dice. That's the life for you, hair shirts and allelujahs.'

She slammed out of the room. He heard her go to the toilet. He knew what she would be doing in there.

Had he been a weaker man he might have cried.

FRIDAY

42 The flat was the top half of a pleasant suburban semi-detached house in Laburnum Road, Southgate.

It was an area inhabited by the aspiring middle class, by those who had put the first foot on the ladder that led to the second car, the second home, the second marriage, the first ulcer. In the main they were busy young people, keeping to themselves, anxious to maintain propriety, determinedly self-contained. No better place in which to remain anonymous.

The downstairs flat of number 31 was leased by a couple at present away working on contract in Zambia. The upper flat had been leased by agents acting for the deceased owner's estate. It had been the agent who had recognized the photofit pictures.

'Such a nice young couple,' he told the police, 'said he was an accountant, she was a secretary in a solicitor's office, absolutely respectable, perhaps you've made a mistake . . .'

But there was no mistake.

Corelli picked up Dice at his house and drove him straight to Laburnum Road.

Detective Inspector Beal had taken charge of the search of the premises. He indicated a briefcase which he had placed on the dining table.

'Found this in the bedroom, sir.'

There were two Australian passports in the names of Arleen Pepper and Grant Hayes. The photographs were of the terrorists. The passports purported to have been issued in Canberra two months before. The girl was described as a secretary, the man as an accountant. There were visas stamped for Hong Kong, Rome, Paris and finally London twelve days previously.

'What d'you think, sir?' Corelli asked, indicating the passports.

'They're very good. Probably genuine.'

'Until our friends got hold of them.'

'Exactly.'

Also in the briefcase were air tickets from London Heathrow to Rome, issued at West London Air Terminal for a flight on the afternoon of the previous Tuesday, the first day of the siege.

'They missed their plane,' said Corelli.

There were 500 American \$10 bills, £50 in English currency and an International Driving Licence in the name of Grant Hayes, issued six days before, in London.

'How is the search going, David?' Dice asked.

'We've been through the place, sir. I wouldn't take it apart until you arrived.'

'Do it now, brick by brick.'

'Yes, sir.'

'Have you tried the G.P.O., David?'

'Yes sir. They didn't make any calls from here. None at all.'

Dice nodded. Beal scurried away to begin the destruction of the flat.

'No weapons,' Corelli said.

'No. They intended to go out clean. I don't suppose the weapons were ever here.'

'Which means they have a contact in this country.'

'Yes. I've no doubt of that.'

'Well, if there's a lead to be had here, our team will find it.'

Corelli drove them to Hampstead. Dice was silent, it was Corelli who eventually spoke.

'These two, they seem very confident, almost as if they think they're going to be rescued.'

'Yes.'

'But that's impossible.'

'Is it?'

Corelli stared at Dice longer than he should have. An irate taxi driver screamed abuse and hit his horn. Corelli steered back on to his own side of the road. Dice seemed not to have noticed the episode.

'Yes, it's impossible,' Corelli said.

'They ripped out the telephone, but they had time to use it first,' Dice reminded him.

'Even so, they'd need an army . . .'

'Perhaps. We've had a lot of success over the years, Ray. I'm sure the enemy have learnt from their mistakes. Those two have been trained in siege tactics, I'm sure of it. Why bother to do that if there is no intention to get them out?'

'String out the siege, maximum publicity I suppose.'

'But nobody claimed this one. We had to find out who it was by devious means. Even now, we can't be absolutely sure we're right. Yet those two are sure, they're sure they're going to come out of this on top. Why?'

'God knows. I still say it's impossible. We're never going to let them out of that flat except to give themselves up and we can't be taken by force.'

'Yet they think it's possible. And they know more than we do.'

With Detective Inspector Beal engaged on the search, Detective Inspector Coates had taken over in the control room. When Dice and Corelli arrived he handed Dice an envelope.

'Ballistics report, sir. And the Commissioner phoned ten minutes ago. I explained what had happened, about finding the flat. He asked you to ring as soon as you returned.'

'Thank you, John.'

The report told them that Alexander Pope and one of the policemen had both been killed by bullets from the same gun. The other police officers had died from bullets from a second but similar weapon. Ballistics thought the weapons were probably Kalashnikov automatic rifles.

'Brilliant!' said Corelli.

Dice telephoned the Commissioner, brought him up to date with the morning news. Then Doctor Tickner buttonholed him.

'Dice, I'm wasting your time and mine being here.'

'Hardly.'

'Don't be polite. All four of them are healthy as horses. Now the hostages are unbound there's no problen, short of getting them out of there. They've got food and water, they could all be in there for another week. Call me if you need me, I'll come at once, okay?'

Dice nodded reluctantly.

'I suppose you're right, Bob. Thanks.'

'I'll leave some pills. If things get really tough, they'll help keep you going.'

'I don't think . . .'

'Don't be daft. They're not addictive. You just might need to stay alert that extra hour.'

They shook hands, then Tickner left. Dice felt unreasonably resentful, as if in some way Tickner had defected. He took the ballistics report into the bedroom to read in peace.

After a while the door opened and Jean Peck walked in. Dice stood up until she had taken a chair.

'You're not leaving us, Jean?' he asked.

'No.'

'You'll need someone to stand in for you now that Bob's gone.'

'No. I'll take my rest, play back the tapes. I've hardly started my part of the job yet. Dice, I'm worried about you.'

'Me?'

'I *am* a doctor.'

'There's nothing wrong with me, Jean.'

'Physically maybe not. I know you're short of sleep, under strain, but it's not just this job, is it? There's something else.'

'I can assure you . . .'

'I'm not asking you to tell *me*. Go to another doctor, but *do* go.'

'A psychiatrist?'

'It could help you, Dice.'

'You know, I always say anyone who goes to see a psychiatrist needs his head examined.'

It was the nearest she had ever known Dice get to a joke. She grinned ruefully.

'Okay. You're a big strong boy. You don't need anyone.'

She stood up, about to leave.

'Jean . . .'

'Yes?'

'Thank you.'

She turned away quickly, lest he should see.

43 CODE E.A.D. 5.J. FROM DIAKENOV EXECUTIVE ACTION DEPARTMENT 1ST CHIEF DIRECTORATE TO KARELIN EX LONDON REFERENTURA.

PINA VOLUNTEERS INFORMATION HIS U.K. CONTACT HUSSEIN BEIDA C/O CASTLE COTTAGE BURSTON VILLAGE TONBRIDGE KENT. BEIDA HOLDS RELIEF PLAN EVENT SIEGE. ALL RISKS ACCEPTABLE ENSURE CARPENTER LIVES. TAKE EXECUTIVE ACTION BEIDA/AGENTS. DESTRUCT NOTICE APPLIES. END.

44 'You wished to see me, sir?'

'Yes, Ben. Do take a seat.'

Deputy Assistant Commissioner Yallop took a chair and waited. Sir John Cowling shuffled papers on his desk for a moment, then looked round his austere modern office before attending to his visitor.

'How is it going, Ben? Give me your estimation.'

'The Spencer Road siege?'

'Yes.'

'I think Dice has real problems this time.'

'He says that?'

'No. That's my opinion.'

'These things are never easy. Why is this case so very different, do you think?'

'They're fanatics, those two.'

'Aren't they all? Isn't it almost an essential element in the terrorist make-up?'

'To a degree. I've not interfered, I've kept well out of the way, but from what I've seen they're particularly dangerous. Dice thinks they have support in this country, I'm inclined to agree with him.'

'But we have them, it's just a matter of time.'

'You've seen them on the monitor?'

'Yes.'

'They're particularly relaxed, more than discipline could account for. I suspect they may try to shoot their way out.'

'And in the last resort, they would kill Carpenter?'

'I think so.'

'They will never give themselves up, you think?'

'I doubt it.'

'Let's hope you're wrong, Ben.'

'For once, I hope so too.'

The Commissioner stared out of his window, across the afternoon rooftops of London.

'There is another matter.'

'Yes, sir?'

'Next January Mr Cottar retires on age limit.'

Yallop sat very still.

'I think he is expecting an extension, sir,' he said, after a moment.

'You think so, Ben?'

'Yes.'

'There will be no extension.'

'I see.'

'You will take over as Assistant Commissioner Crime when he leaves.'

'Very well, sir.'

'I am looking to the future, Ben. I want a younger man available when Mr Collins, the Deputy Commissioner, retires in eighteen months. I think my immediate deputy should be a younger man, someone in touch with the thinking and feeling of the junior officers. As A.C.C. you would be well placed for consideration for his post. After that, it is rather up to you.'

'I'm obliged, sir.'

'All this is strictly *entre nous*, of course.'

Yallop walked down the corridor, his brain swimming in delighted confusion. It is not every day a man is given the promise of his heart's desire in quite such an unequivocal manner.

45 Firth ordered a whisky and soda.

The barman wore a pink blouse and gold pendant earrings. He returned with the order as Maztikyan appeared at the bar.

'Here you are, luv,' said the barman, 'what's your friend having?'

Firth smiled an enquiry.

'Vodka and tonic, please,' Maztikyan said in a deliberate deep brown voice.

The barman dimpled prettily and turned away. Firth noticed that Maztikyan seemed ill at ease.

'Anything wrong?' he enquired.

The Russian looked round the small, crowded saloon bar. In this company the precious barman was likely to feel very much at home. There were no women present. A heady waft of scent imposed itself above the smell of alcohol and tobacco smoke.

'Nothing,' Maztikyan said.

The barman placed the vodka and tonic beside Firth's whisky. Firth paid.

'Thank you,' he said.

'Pleasure, dear,' said the barman.

Firth led the way to a corner near the window.

'Nice little pub,' he said.

'Yes.'

'Cheers, old chap.'

'Your good health,' said Maztikyan.

'What's new?' Firth asked after they had sipped.

The Russian looked round the room. All were engrossed in their own sub-world, talking loudly, spicing the talk with laughter, sometimes gruff, sometimes trilling.

He handed Firth a copy of the message from Diakenov to Karelin. Firth read it.

'This could be awkward,' Firth said.

'Not necessarily. I suggest you let Karelin go ahead.'

'I can hardly do that, old chap.'

'Why not? He will get more out of Beida than your people could. He doesn't have your . . . restrictions.'

'True.'

'What he learns, I will learn. I can then pass it on.'

'Mmmm . . .'

'What can you lose? If it goes well everyone will be happy. If it goes wrong, no blame attaches to your department.'

'It must not go wrong. We must have Carpenter alive.'

'Karelin is an expert. You know that.'

'True, but you cannot guarantee he will succeed.'

'Nor can you guarantee that your police will succeed. You have read Karelin's instructions, he is to ensure Carpenter is released alive.'

Firth thought quickly. There was a good deal to recommend the course of action that Maztikyan proposed. It mattered little whether he was telling the truth or not, but on balance Firth thought he probably was.

'We'll leave it like that then,' he said.

'Good.'

'Care for another?'

'My turn, I think.'

'How kind.'

'Roger . . . a favour?'

'Of course, dear boy.'

'From now on I would prefer it if I were the one to select the places where we meet.'

'Really?' said Firth.

'Really.'

46 At 9 p.m. the telephone rang in the control room. Detective Inspector Coates answered and handed the receiver to Dice.

'For you sir, David Beal.'

'Yes, David?'

'Nothing, sir. We've taken this flat apart but there's absolutely nothing else there.'

'Very well, David. Call it off.'

'I'm sorry sir. We could try again.'

'Don't concern yourself, David. If there had been anything to find you would have found it.'

He told Corelli.

'So we still don't know their real names,' Corelli said.

'It's not so important, the names. We know as much about them as we need. We can identify them by numbers for all the difference it makes now.'

'I thought that was what we tore the flat apart for.'

'No. I hoped for a lead to their contact in this country, if we could grab him or her, then they might be prepared to talk.'

'You think so? I was rather glad we couldn't tell them the K.G.B. have got Pina. If they expect help from outside and we block that avenue, they might shoot their way out, try to.'

'It would be up to us to obviate that. Anyway, since we have no lead on the contact the question doesn't arise.'

On the monitor the terrorists and their hostages had just finished a meal. But for the guns it was a peaceful enough scene.

Jean Peck stood up and joined them.

'Have you noticed how they check their watches against the radio time signal at least twice a day?' she asked.

'They expect some attempt to rescue them, Jean,' said Dice.

'I know, I've heard you talking about it. The point is, I think we can say that they know exactly when that rescue attempt will be made. They know the day and the hour, the minute.'

'I think you're right,' said Dice.

'Also, they've split up the day into sections and they stick to their routine. They eat, sleep, exercise, take recreation at the same times, like clockwork.'

'Does that have some significance?' Corelli asked.

'It shows tremendous discipline. I think they must have been in this situation before, or rehearsed it. They know exactly what they're doing, the routine they've adopted helps them avoid the mental and physical pitfalls of their situation. Even so, I think the man is wilting.'

Dice was suddenly alert.

'What makes you think that, Jean?'

'He has developed a habit of letting his right arm fall loose and flicking his thumb against the palm of his hand. It's a not unusual nervous gesture. Also he's on the move a good deal, not settling in one spot or one position for long. He's getting the jitters.'

'How does that relate to the suggestion that they know exactly when to expect a rescue attempt?' Dice asked.

'I think it must still be some way off.'

'How long?'

'I can't answer that, Dice.'

'Days, hours?'

'Not hours . . .'

'Maybe he's getting edgy because it's getting near time,' Corelli put in.

'I don't think so. Near to the time I would expect a different reaction. As much as anything he's probably fretting at a lack of action and because there is no immediate prospect of seeing any.'

On the monitor the occupants of the room had finished their meal, used the portable toilet and settled back into their agreed positions, the hostages on the floor, the terrorists in armchairs.

The man had let his arm hang loose over the side of his armchair and was flicking his thumb against his palm in a constant monotonous jerky movement.

'He's at it again,' said Corelli.

The girl got up and moved across the room, bent down and whispered into the man's ear. He half grinned, looked uncertain. She whispered again. He stood up and together they moved her armchair round so that its back faced the hostages.

'Now what?' said Corelli.

The girl sat in the armchair, pulled up her skirt and pushed her pants and tights down to her ankles in brazen show. The man was fumbling at the front of his trousers. The girl opened her legs and held up her arms for him. He knelt down in front of her and she pulled him forward.

'My God! . . . they're . . .' Corelli stumbled to a halt.

The man had his head buried in the girl's shoulder, his body was moving urgently. The girl lay still, stroking the back of his head as if he were a child come for comfort, acquiescing in the act but barely participating.

'Clever bitch!' said Jean.

'You think she knew?' Dice asked.

'She knew.'

'Bloody animals . . . !' said Corelli.

'You're a prude, Ray,' Jean said.

'I'm not! But doing it in front of people, only animals do that!'

'They are not aware that we're watching,' said Dice.

'I mean Carpenter and the girl.'

'They turned the chair round.'

But Corelli had forgotten his disgust, another thought had come.

'Dice, if we could only get a couple of chaps on to that balcony now . . .'

'She's facing the french windows, her gun's beside the armchair on the floor, would you want to be first down the rope?'

The man had collapsed forward on to the girl, holding her in a clumsy embrace. After a moment she pushed him off and adjusted her dress.

'Next client please, the show must go on,' said Corelli acidly.

'That wasn't a show, Ray,' Dice said.

'No, that was therapy,' said Jean.

47 It was midnight when Dice arrived home. He had left the control room much against his will but the combined arguments of Corelli and Jean Peck had finally worn him down.

He had a feeling, and he had learnt to trust such feelings, that the climax was approaching. But not quite yet, not tonight.

As he had expected, the house was in darkness and once inside he was alone. He felt guilty because he was glad that Betty was not there. They had been married just five years, four of which had been torture for him, probably for her as well. He had been widowed seven years when they met, his first marriage had been childless but happy, and he was not the cold man he seemed, not a man to be alone.

Dice lived yet in the hope that he and Betty might find an acceptable compromise, a way of coexistence that did not involve hurt pride and bitter resentment. He was a man of considerable loyalty, one to accept his responsibilities, even when they became onerous. He prayed often, not for release from the punishing strain of their relationship but for Betty's happiness. God knows it was not her fault, the way she was.

He poured himself a drink and sat in an armchair in the lounge, staring into space, surrounded by the records and record covers his wife had abandoned the night before and left, with the overful ashtray and the dirty crockery, to fend for themselves.

Dice felt desperately tired, emotionally drained. He discovered that his glass was empty but could not remember drinking. He poured himself another, set it on the arm of the chair beside him.

He fell asleep.

Betty came home just after 2 a.m. She was wearing a tight

dress cut low at the front. Her makeup and her hair were in disarray. She was moderately drunk.

'Hell, Dice! You're that tired, go to bed.'

She found the bottle, poured herself a drink.

Dice came to with a start, momentarily uncertain of his surroundings.

Betty giggled, dumped herself into an armchair opposite him, spilling the drink on to her dress. She swore quietly to herself, opened her legs to brush the liquid off her dress. And Dice was back in the control room, watching the girl terrorist make herself available, not because of physical need but because it was expedient.

'I meant to go to bed, I fell asleep,' Dice said.

He wished now he had gone to bed earlier. He hated seeing her like this.

'You can go . . . we can go to bed . . . you're quite safe Dice, you won't be called on tonight . . . it's been done for you.'

She wanted to hurt him. When she was like this she always wanted to hurt him. He understood why.

'Big man, Dice. He really did a good job, really did.'

She stretched luxuriously, as if reliving the moment, but her eyes watched him.

'I'm not getting into a fight, Betty. In the morning . . .'

She sat suddenly upright.

'In the morning when I'm not drunk?' she shouted. 'In the morning when I'm not drunk I might not tell you what a shit you are.'

Dice stood up.

'I'm going to bed.'

'Running away, Dice? Like always?'

'If you say so.'

'Don't bloody patronize me! I'm your wife, I'm telling you I've just had it with another man, don't you bloody *care*?'

'It's happened before.'

'And it'll bloody happen again. He was in the job, Dice, one of your young strapping coppers, how'd you like that? God I've had some policemen, big ones, small ones, ugly ones, beautiful ones . . . Dice . . . they all know about your cow of a wife, they all pity you . . .'

'You're drunk, Betty.'

She threw the drink away, stood to face him, blazing anger.

'It's true, Dice! It's every word true! I'm a whore, I'd have anyone, any way, any time. It's well known. Why don't you *do* something, why don't you hit me, for God's sake *hit* me, Dice.'

'What good would that do?'

He was desolate, quite unable to help her.

Then she collapsed into his arms, her body convulsed with shuddering sobs. He held her, uncertain what to do or say. After a while she quietened, looked up into his face.

'You must get rid of me, Dice. I'm no good for you.'

'I can't do that. I love you.'

'No, you don't. It's duty, loyalty, what the Church says about marriage . . . you're strong on those things. You can't love a shit like me.'

'You feel remorse, that's all.'

'But I'll do it again, Dice. Probably tomorrow, a different man. I know what I am, so do you. I'm a nympho, Dice. It's a disease, I'm hooked like a junkie, you understand that?'

'Yes, I understand.'

'And I hooked you, deliberately. God, I wanted you! But if you'd known, you'd never have married me. What it cost me, Dice, what it cost me to keep it from you. I was burning for you but I had to stop myself. I don't know how I did it. You have to get rid of me, for your own sake.'

'We can look at this thing together Betty, now it's in the open, we can fight it together . . .'

'No, Dice. I'll only end up destroying you. See what happened tonight? I have to blame *you* for it. I get so disgusted with myself, I can't bear to blame myself, I have to blame you, make out it's your fault.'

'There's no question of blame, Betty . . .'

'There is. Not for what I'm like, for what I *did*, tricking you into marrying me, there's blame for that.'

She broke away from him, looked round the room.

'Go to bed, Dice. I'm going to clean up this place. No reason you should come home to a whore *and* a pigsty.'

'Betty, if only you believed . . .'

She laughed, a short, bitter, nerve-jingling noise.

'Don't joke, Dice. Your God, if he's up there, your God made me, made me what I am, and you and I are both suffering for it. Go to bed, leave me alone. I'm not drunk any more. I just want to get this place cleaned up. Call it atonement.'

Dice went to the bedroom. Later, Betty joined him. She undressed, got into bed, turned away from him and was apparently soon asleep.

Dice lay awake for a long time. He had problems at work but at least they were clear cut. He was on the side of good, the terrorists on the side of evil. Here at home there were no such clear divisions. There were only grey amorphous areas of undefined guilt, felt but in part denied. He could not see ahead. He felt himself empty, a husk discarded by the machinery of life.

Eli, Eli, Lema Sabachthani? My God, my God, why have you forsaken me?

Never had it been more difficult for Dice to hang on to his faith. How hard to find God, how easy to lose him.

SATURDAY

48 At 5 a.m., before it was light, Paul Carpenter woke. Beside him, Mary Tü slept fitfully, making tiny disturbed noises, muscles flickering against the discomfort of the hard floor and the tension that was present even in sleep.

Across the room the man had turned away from them, playing solitaire on a low table by the half light of the floodlights. The girl was asleep on the settee, bundled up in blankets.

Carpenter edged closer to Mary Tü, until he lay beside her. He placed his hand gently over her mouth and whispered into her ear, so low that it was no more than a breath.

'Mary . . .'

She stirred, went still under his restraining hand.

'You must be very quiet, listen to what I say. If you hear and understand, nod your head. Do not speak.'

He felt the girl nod.

'Mary, these people intend to kill me . . .'

She moved, he tightened his hand on her mouth.

'No, listen. That is why they came here, to kill Alex and me. You heard the radio, you know it's true. You must be brave, I don't think they will harm you . . .'

The terrorist grunted in annoyance, pushed the cards together on the table, shuffled and dealt them. Carpenter waited until the man had settled, then spoke again.

'They intend to destroy the Party, Mary. They hope to destroy the whole idea. We must *not* allow that to happen. There are others who can replace Alex and me, you understand?'

She was silent for a moment, then nodded.

'Tell Stephen he is to take over as General Secretary, you are to be his personal assistant. There will be a wave of public sympathy for us, you must use that. Tell Stephen there will be no better time, we must put up candidates in every ward in next year's election. You must obtain the maximum publicity for our deaths. You will be asked what my last words to you were, tell them I said this: No social order can stand for long unless it takes account of God, and of the spirituality of his children. Praise God for his gift of free will, work and give of yourselves for his cause, forgive those whose ignorance of Him leads them to dark deeds. Can you remember that, Mary?'

She did not move. Carpenter repeated the words slowly and carefully. Then Mary nodded. Then she took his hand, kissed it, and placed it on the top of her head.

'God bless and keep you, today and evermore,' Carpenter said.

He moved away. The girl made no sound, but he knew that she was crying.

49 At 10 a.m. the watchers in the control room saw the man take the landline telephone and seconds later it rang in the room. Dice answered.

'This is Commander Dice.'

'We want another toilet,' the man said.

'Very well.'

'And more food, the same as before but something hot as well.'

'And in return?' Dice asked.

'In return the hostages stay alive.'

'Not much of a bargain, is it?'

'It's all you'll get.'

The girl had moved across to stand beside her fellow terrorist, she was listening.

'The help you are expecting won't arrive,' Dice said.
The girl grabbed the receiver.
'What're you talking about, Dice?'
'You are expecting outside help. I think I should tell you that it will not arrive.'
'Dice, we still want that plane.'
'Do you?'
'You know damn fine well we do. Get it. In the meantime send in the stuff we asked for or the hostages get tied up again.'
She slammed down the receiver.
'I don't think she believed you, Dice,' Jean Peck said.
'I don't think she did.'
'Do we send in the stuff, sir?' Corelli asked.
'Yes, but not yet.'
The terrorists were in a huddle, talking furiously, but nothing came over the audio surveillance equipment.
'The boy is worried again,' said Jean.
'They didn't set a deadline,' Corelli commented.
'They don't have to,' Dice said.
On the monitor the girl made a flat gesture with her hand, terminating the discussion.
'She didn't threaten to kill the hostages either,' Jean said.
Dice was staring at the monitor.
'But she still intends to,' he said.

50 Sir John Cowling arrived at 10.20 a.m. He watched the monitor for a while but there was no activity of interest and he went with Dice into the bedroom.
'They've made contact again, taken more food, that must be a good sign?'
'Perhaps, sir.'
'You don't think so?'
'It's a good sign as far as it goes. They haven't set another deadline for the aircraft either, nor have they made any further threats against the lives of the hostages.'

'Then perhaps they're just stringing it out, putting off the evil hour.'

'No. They have something in mind. I'd like to double the number of S.A.S. men over here.'

The Commissioner was suddenly alarmed.

'You think they'll try to break out?'

'They might. It would help if I could tell them the K.G.B. have detained their boss, Pina.'

'We can't do that.'

'I thought Carpenter's life was top priority, sir.'

'It is.'

'But I am hampered in trying to preserve it.'

'We all have our masters. The Prime Minister must look to the future. Carpenter is vitally important but there might be a next time, someone even more important, we must protect the source of our information.'

'Next time it could be the Prime Minister himself?'

'Anything is possible.'

'He may not have that problem after next year.'

'Oh?'

'If the Christian Democrats put enough candidates up at the next election they'll walk in, after this show, they'll walk in.'

'That had occurred to me.'

'What price Carpenter's life then?'

'I thought I made it clear that Carpenter's life is absolutely top priority. However, we still cannot risk the informant being exposed.'

'The girl intends to kill Carpenter, come what may.'

'You can't be absolutely sure of that, Allan. I grant you that it is likely, but you cannot be absolutely sure.'

'I cannot offer any guarantees for his life, especially not if I can't use all the information I have. The only hope is to convince them that their entire organization is defunct, even then they would probably still kill him. They're fanatics.'

'I'm sorry, Allan. The answer is no.'

The Commissioner left. Dice went into the control room and

telephoned his home number. There was no answer. He then telephoned Deputy Assistant Commissioner Yallop at his office and asked for the extra S.A.S. men. Then he sat down to watch the monitor.

Corelli had been absent from the room. He returned and took his seat beside Dice.

'The food and the replacement toilet are ready, sir,' he said.

'Let them wait a while,' said Dice.

51 Genardy Karelin got off the train at Tonbridge Station at 11.15 a.m. and took a taxi from the forecourt.

He was not conspicuous. His manner of dress and his modern gold-rimmed spectacles gave him the look of a prosperous young executive. He carried a small hide briefcase. He spoke perfect English with just a hint of an American accent.

The taxi took him to the small village of Hadlow, where he paid off the driver. He was faced with a four-mile walk but that was nothing to him.

When he reached Burston village he spent some time wandering round, looking for Castle Cottage, not wishing to ask for the location. He found it a quarter-mile outside the village itself, an old rambling building set in an expensive five acres.

Karelin went straight to the front door and rang the bell. After a while, receiving no answer, he walked round to the back of the house. The kitchen and lounge doors were locked and there was no sign of the inhabitant.

He went to the integral garage and discovered it to be empty, then returned to the rear garden, found a wooden seat in a secluded spot, and sat down.

From his briefcase he took a bar of chocolate, broke off a square and placed it carefully in his mouth.

He was content to wait.

52 The portable toilet and the food arrived on the balcony of the siege flat just after 12 noon, lowered from the roof and left for the terrorists to collect.

The girl motioned to Carpenter with her rifle.

'Go get it.'

She pushed the french windows open, stood back covering him and he went out on to the balcony. He collected the packages of food and drink and brought them back into the room, then returned to the balcony.

As he bent down to pick up the metal toilet, something caught Carpenter's eye, a flash of silver against the front wall of the building. He hesitated for several seconds, staring at the flexible metal tubing before he realized that it might have to do with the police observation of the flat. He clasped the toilet in his arms, walked back into the room and placed it on the floor.

The girl grabbed him by his shirt front, jammed the barrel of her rifle into his neck. She spoke out loud.

'What is it? What did you see?'

Carpenter said nothing.

53 The moment they saw Carpenter out on the balcony, staring at the metal piping of the television camera eye, the watchers knew they had problems.

'Oh, no!' Corelli groaned.

They watched on the monitor as the girl grabbed Carpenter and threatened him with the gun.

'What was it? What did you see?'

Her voice boomed out across the control room from the audio equipment left permanently on high volume to pick up the least sound.

Carpenter stood still, his head hung down, angry at his own stupidity.

'You want to die, Carpenter?'

'No.'

'Tell me, no lies mind . . .'

'I will not lie, nor will I tell you.'

'Oh, hell!' Jean Peck exclaimed.

'He can do nothing else,' said Dice.

The girl threw Carpenter away from her.

'You've told me enough,' she said.

The other terrorist stood threatening the hostages with his rifle as the girl dropped to the floor and squirmed her way out on to the balcony. The watchers went to the window.

'They could get her, Dice. The S.A.S. chaps could pick her off,' Corelli said.

Dice pointed at the monitor, at the terrorist threatening Carpenter with the rifle.

'And him, could they kill him as well?'

The girl rolled on to her back, staring up at the wall of the siege building. Her rifle came up and she sprayed a hail of automatic fire at the thin flexible metal piping.

The monitor screen suddenly went blank.

Dice watched grim-faced through the telescope as the girl scrabbled back through the french windows and the curtains were pulled hastily across.

Seconds later her voice blasted into the room.

'Dice, you bastard! I know you can hear me. That was your last bloody chance.'

Then the room was suddenly full of gunfire, then there was silence.

'She shot out the bloody bug!' said Corelli, stating the obvious.

'Where's Mr Delabole?' Dice asked.

'In the command van.'

'Tell him to replace it, quickly!'

'Yes, sir.'

Corelli ran from the room.

Dice slumped into a chair. Jean stood looking at him, concerned at the desperation in his eyes.

'Dice . . .'

'Yes?'

'There's still hope . . .'

'Yes, there's always hope.'

Then she too slumped.

'We're in trouble, aren't we?'
'We always were.'

54 At 4 p.m. Hussein Beida arrived home at Castle Cottage. He garaged his car and entered the house by the front door. The moment the door was open he felt the cold circle of a gun muzzle on the back of his neck.

'Enter the house, Beida. Move slowly. Keep your hands where I can see them.'

Faced with the inevitable, he did as he was told.

'Go into the dining room,' Karelin ordered.

Beida did so. In the room, he was about to speak when the butt of the gun descended on the back of his skull. He was unconscious before he hit the floor.

Karelin stripped the body naked, then laid it on the dining table, face up. He went to the kitchen and after a brief search returned with a length of plastic-covered washing line. He tied an end to Beida's left wrist, passed the line under the table and tied it to the right wrist, pulling the cord tight before running it down under the table and repeating the operation with Beida's ankles. He used the remainder of the line to secure the body at the neck, chest and stomach, rendering his victim immobile.

Beida was spread-eagled across the table, legs apart, unable to move, as vulnerable as a man can be. Karelin sat down in a chair to wait.

When Beida finally returned to full consciousness he was instantly afraid. His captor stood over him, watching his face with apparent anxiety, as a surgeon might regard a patient after a particularly dangerous experimental operation.

'Who are you, what do you want?' Beida mumbled.

He tried to raise his head but the cord bit into his neck, threatening to throttle him.

'I want you to talk to me,' Karelin said.

He held up a gas lighter, showed it to Beida. He moved the flame regulator to 'high', stabbed at the igniter button. The flame was about two inches long, yellow at the top, then faint blue, invisible white at the base. He held the lighter close to Beida's ear. The hissing of the flame filled his head and he smelt his hair burning.

'What d'you want, man?' Beida yelled.

But Karelin had moved out of sight, was standing at the foot of the table, between Beida's open legs. He had clicked off the lighter when he moved, but now Beida heard another click and that terrifying hissing sound again. His body writhed under his bonds.

'Talk to me, Beida,' Karelin said.

'What? What about?' Beida shouted desperately.

'I think you know. In order to jog your memory I intend to fry your testicles.'

Blind panic coursed through Beida's brain, blotting out rational thought, rendering him momentarily mute. He smelt his pubic hair burning, then there was sudden excruciating pain, pain beyond belief, beyond bearing.

Beida screamed.

Then he talked.

Then Karelin shot him dead.

55 There were two brooms kept in a cupboard in the kitchen area of the siege flat. The terrorists had already used one to pull the landline receiver in from the balcony, the other the man now found and brought into the living area together with the ball of twine.

After the discovery of the T.V. eye, the hostages had been re-gagged and their arms bound, but they had not been tied at the ankles. The girl intended they should retain a degree of mobility.

She took the two brooms and bound them together with the twine so that they formed a rough 'T' shape.

From the holdall the man took eight packets of plastic explosive, eight detonators, wire, insulating tape and a small battery, still wrapped in its protective plastic covering.

Using the twine, he strung the packets of P.E. and the battery together in a line, forming a lethal necklace. He then forced a $1\frac{1}{2}$-inch detonator into each packet and joined them and the battery with the wire. He was left with two ends of twine to tie the necklace into position and two bare ends of wire which, when touched, would complete the electrical circuit and detonate the bomb.

For the moment he bound the bare ends of the wire with insulating tape, a premature explosion was no part of the plan.

The hostages watched the operation with mounting apprehension, aware that no good for them could come of it and that the manufacture of the bomb heralded the climax of their detention. It was now clear to Mary Tü that Carpenter had been right, she no longer had the slightest doubt that the terrorists intended to kill her priest and that the end of this affair would be violent and bloody.

It took the man an hour and a half to complete the task to his satisfaction. Having done it, he placed the device carefully on the sideboard and covered it with one of the cartons which had contained food sent in by the police.

When he had finished, he took over guard and the girl selected food for them. She did not bother to feed the hostages; there was no longer any point in doing that.

Carpenter had already had his last supper.

56 Commander Dice worried his way through the day.

The watchers were now blind, although hearing had been restored when Delabole's men had replaced the bug on the door of the siege room.

They heard very little. Not one word of clear speech, just occasional muted whisperings and quiet unidentifiable noises.

Dice sensed they were near the climax and that the discovery of the television camera had little or nothing to do with it. He knew the terrorists planned action but he could not imagine what they might have in mind. The enemy had kept the initiative throughout, they still had it, and he could do nothing but wait. The frustration was a constant nagging pain, the fear of what was to come was like the dead mental ache of a terminal illness.

And throughout the day his mind turned again and again to his wife. He telephoned several times but received no answer.

By 9 p.m. the watchers, except for Dice, had become somewhat adjusted to the new situation. It was hard not to be deceived by the silence, the inactivity. The acute tension of the moment when the television camera had been shot out had drained away, dissipated by time.

At 9.30 p.m. Dice, torn by conflicting loyalties, came to a decision. He had his car called, was driven home, told the driver to wait.

The house was tidy, spotlessly clean. On the kitchen table was a large cardboard box full of groceries. On the table beside the box was the letter, a single sheet of paper, folded over, pinned to the table by a can of baked beans.

There was no heading to the letter, nor was it signed. It was as if she were in the room, talking to him. It said: 'I had to do it because you never would have. Do *yourself* a kindness for once, divorce me. You have ample grounds.' That was all.

In the car, heading back towards Hampstead, Dice felt cold, alone, dead inside.

SUNDAY

57 The noises were first heard in the control room at 4.30 a.m.

Detective Inspector Beal was on night duty. At first he was undecided whether he was justified in waking his senior officers or not. Then, above the vague bumpings, scufflings and the occasional metallic clink, he heard the girl laugh, low and intense and excited.

He called Dice and Corelli, played back the noises for them on the tape recorder.

'Call Jean,' Dice told Corelli.

Jean Peck wore a dressing-gown over her nightdress but still shivered in the early morning cold as she listened to the tape.

Dice and Corelli dressed rapidly and returned to the control room.

'What do you think?' Dice asked the psychiatrist.

She looked at him, tired, sad.

'I can't help you any more, Dice. If this was a western I'd tell you to go and get your gun.'

'Ray?'

'They didn't get up at this time in the morning to pick flowers.'

'I agree. Alert the S.A.S. Call the command van, I want every man we have out of his bed and ready for action.'

Corelli grabbed at the telephone.

Dice went to the window. It was still dark, faint streaks of dawn in the sky. For the moment there was nothing to see but the buildings of Spencer Road illuminated by the floodlights.

'I'm going to get dressed, Dice,' Jean said.

Dice did not answer, he was still staring out of the window. She left.

Corelli had the disposition map in front of him and was barking staccato orders into the telephone. The urgency, the expectancy and the tension had returned to the room.

But still nothing happened.

Jean Peck returned after fifteen minutes, dressed, her face made up. Corelli had replaced the telephone but thereafter it rang intermittently, officers reporting themselves in position.

At 5 a.m. the terrorists' voices intruded suddenly into the room.

'Ready?' The girl.

'Sure.' The man.

'Let's go.' The girl again.

The curtains behind the french windows of the siege flat suddenly parted, the doors opened and four figures appeared on the balcony.

So bizarre, so shockingly unexpected was the scene now revealed to the watchers that it stunned them into silent immobility.

The hostages were in front, the terrorists part hidden behind them. Mary Tü had her hands tied behind her back; behind her, covered by her body, was the girl terrorist and she carried her gun slung over her shoulder, held the landline receiver in her hands. Her male colleague was beside her, menacing the hostages with the automatic rifle in his left hand, his right hand holding two wires separated by the width of two of his fingers.

Paul Carpenter stood beside Mary Tü. It was his condition that caused the debilitating shock in the control room. His arms were stretched out to his sides, bound on to the shaft of a broom. Another broom handle tied on to the first to form a 'T' shape, projected above his head and ran down his back and to this he was bound at the waist, chest and neck. Around his forehead, tied into position by the twine, a parody of a crown, was the string of explosives. It was from the bomb around Carpenter's head that the two wires held by the male terrorist emanated.

The frozen tableau in the control room lasted bare seconds that seemed like a lifetime.

Dice moved first, leaping for the telescope, aiming it in on the group on the balcony.

'Is it a bomb?' Jean Peck asked in a hushed whisper.

'It's a bomb,' said Dice.

58 The girl waited a few seconds, giving the watchers time to appreciate the hopelessness of their position.

The idea to crown Carpenter with explosive had been hers. It had tickled her limited sense of humour. He was a priest, wasn't he? He should be honoured.

When she judged that enough time had passed, that Dice would be watching, she picked up the landline receiver and depressed the call button.

They answered immediately. She did not give them time to talk.

'I want a car in front of this house immediately. Full tank, no bugs.'

'I can't do that,' said a voice.

'Dice?'

'Yes.'

'This is it. This is the end. We're quite prepared to die. Send the car now.'

'You know that's impossible. Perhaps there's some other way . . .'

'No. You want convincing?'

She nodded to the man. He pushed Carpenter forward, urged him up on to the parapet of the balcony. Carpenter, awkwardly constrained, swayed perilously on the edge of the drop. Behind him the man displayed the bare ends of the wire, but never lost control of his rifle.

'You see, Dice?'

'Yes.'

'Take down the barrier to my left. Reverse the car in. Do it right now.'

'It will take time, getting a car, taking down the barrier, can't we . . .'

'You have five minutes.'

'That's not long enough . . .'

'It's all you're getting. Five minutes. Dice . . .?'

'Yes?'

'Bring the car yourself. You drive it personally, understand?'

She threw the landline over the balcony, signalling the end of the conversation. It hung down the face of the building, swinging from side to side, twisting as it bounced off the wall.

The decision to tell Dice to bring the car himself had been a last-minute thing. She suddenly wanted to see what he looked like. She was essentially female, curious to meet this enemy whose professionalism almost matched her own.

What *sort* of man was he, this Dice?

59 'You can't do it, sir.'

'I have no choice, Ray.'

'You have. They've never seen you. Someone else could go, they'd never know the difference.'

'*I* would.'

'Dice, let *me* go.'

'No.'

'Then ask for a volunteer.'

'No.'

'But they'll kill you . . .'

'Perhaps. More reason for not sending someone else. Inspector Beal, order one section of the hoarding by the command van to be removed and my car to be made ready by the gap.'

'Yes, sir.'

'D'you *want* to die?' asked Jean Peck, resenting his determination.

'No, Jean. My chances of survival are somewhat better than those of the hostages.'

'You may be psychologically unfit to go.'

'A professional opinion?'

Dice looked at his watch. He had three minutes.

'Yes. You've been showing signs of acute strain these last two days. Your judgement could be affected. Dice, I am of the opinion that you don't really care if you live or die at the moment. You could make a simple but fatal error because of that, fatal not just for you but also for the hostages.'

'I don't agree. I do not intend to commit suicide. But I am not appalled by the prospect of death.'

'You're a fool!'

She turned away, a bitter loser.

'Jean . . . I shall take the greatest care.'

'Like hell!'

'You have my word. Even if I wanted to, I could not commit suicide.'

'Your damn God, I suppose!'

'Yes. But He may intend I die. If that is so, it does not trouble me, nothing in this life is as good as we remember it, nothing so bad as we anticipate it will be.'

But at that moment Jean Peck had no interest in Dice's philosophy of life, only the preservation of his body.

Dice turned to Corelli.

'Follow my car. Take one of our men and two S.A.S. marksmen with you. A back-up team follows you but you must all stay out of sight. Get me a lapel microphone, you should be able to stay near enough to pick up a clear signal.'

'They might search you . . .'

'I don't think so, they're in too much of a hurry. I'll take that chance.'

Corelli picked up the telephone.

'Inspector Beal . . .' Dice said.

'Sir?'

'Telephone the Commissioner, acquaint him with the situation. Then call the D.A.C. Ops. You have control of the office until Mr Yallop or the Commissioner arrives.'

'Yes, sir.'

'No one is to enter the flat. It may be booby-trapped.'

Dice walked out of the room. He said goodbye to nobody. He had one minute left.

60 The girl was not absolutely sure she had won until the centre section of the street barricade began to come down. She felt no sense of relief, she had been quite prepared to carry out her threat, detonate the bomb and kill everyone on the balcony, herself included.

None the less, it had been a long five minutes. She signalled to the man and he pulled Paul Carpenter down from the parapet.

Mary Tü was standing absolutely still, eyes wide open, her body quivering with shock.

A car backed into the street through the opening in the barricade. It reversed slowly and came to a stop outside the siege house. A man got out, stood clear of the car in the centre of the roadway and looked up at the balcony, hands on hips, as if critically surveying the property with a view to purchase.

'Dice?' the girl called down to him.

She did not doubt who he was, he looked the part, looked much as she had expected. The casually elegant clothes, the assumption of superiority, the aura of controlled efficiency.

'Yes,' Dice replied.

'Clear your men out of this building,' she demanded.

'They have already gone,' he called up.

His voice was cold, factual and remote, with no detectable accent. She believed him.

'Stay where you are, we're coming down.'

She saw him nod.

They retreated into the siege room and the man removed the

desk from in front of the door. They formed into a line; Carpenter first, then the man, gun in one hand and bare wires from the bomb in the other; then the girl and Mary Tü close up behind them.

In this fashion they entered the hall of the flat and walked to the front door. There was no sign of police activity.

'Okay. Go on,' the girl said.

They made their way down to the ground floor.

Carpenter, his arms held out at right angles to his body, had difficulty in negotiating the stairs. The man forced him along, holding him where the broomsticks were linked together in the centre of his back.

At the front door of the building the man stopped, unable to see down the road beyond the high wooden barricade.

'I can't see anything,' he said.

'Go on then,' the girl urged.

'I mean, you can't see for those bloody fences they've put up.'

'Get a move on,' the girl commanded, 'we'll be late. They won't try anything.'

Somewhat reluctantly the man pushed Carpenter ahead.

Dice stood apart from the car. It seemed that he had not moved.

'Go right up to him,' the girl ordered.

When they were close to Dice, the girl pushed Mary Tü alongside Carpenter so that the man could cover her, then turned her gun on Dice.

'Hands against the car,' she ordered.

Dice walked to the car, leant forward and placed his hands on the roof. The girl searched him quickly.

'I am not armed,' he said.

'Is the car bugged,' she asked.

'No,' Dice replied truthfully.

'Get in the driving seat.'

She jerked her thumb at the man and their hostages, opened the rear door for them. They forced Mary Tü down on to the floor in the back of the car, then manoeuvred Paul Carpenter into the rear seat. The man sat beside him, his gun on his lap, the wires still held in his hand.

The girl got into the front passenger seat. She looked at Dice.

'I hope you've not been stupid,' she said.

'Meaning?'

His eyes were cold blue, vacant, evincing no fear.

'The first sign of interference, we all die.'

'I believe you.'

'Drive.'

Dice started the engine, drove towards the barricade.

'In which direction?'

'Turn right into Willow Road.'

'Then?'

'I'll tell you.'

The press had been caught on the hop by the sudden developments of the last ten minutes. Even so, they manned every vantage point as Dice drove out from behind the barricade, cameras flashing dully in the first light of dawn. Up on a scaffold gantry a television news cameraman pointed his mechanical eye at them, recording their departure for public consumption. A line of uniformed policemen, backs to the car, kept the press at bay, leaving the car a broad avenue of escape into Willow Road.

'Left or right?' Dice asked when they reached the junction with Heath Road.

'Straight across,' the girl said.

Facing them across the road was Hampstead Heath. Immediately opposite was a gravel car park, now occupied by the caravans, stalls and pleasure engines of the visiting fair.

'Into the fairground?'

For the first time Dice sounded faintly disconcerted.

'There's a road through the middle, take it.'

'But it only leads straight on to the Heath. It goes nowhere.'

'Just do as you're told, Dice.'

The girl was enjoying herself. In the end it had all been so very easy.

Dice waited for a milk float to clank and clatter past the front of them, heading downhill towards South End Green, then drove across the road, taking the tarmac path between the sleeping caravans.

'It's not too late,' Dice said.

'To give ourselves up?'

'Yes.'

'Why should we? We're going free.'

'Are you?'

'Bet on it.'

'I don't think I will. I told you, this rescue, it won't happen.'

'We'll see, won't we? You'd just better hope it does, you know the alternative. Turn right here, between the ponds.'

The path had narrowed, was now hard-packed earth, rising up beyond the ponds to a tree-lined ridge near the centre of the Heath.

'Why commit suicide? If I'm right, if you cannot escape, why not cut your losses?'

'We've already won, Dice. No matter what happens, we can't lose.'

'You'd die for a political idea?'

'Yes. Wouldn't you?'

'For a truth, yes. For an idea, especially a political idea, no.'

'Carpenter would.'

'He would die for his religious beliefs perhaps, for God, not for his political ideology, except that he believes that to be inspired by God.'

'Never heard such crap.'

'Freedom has always been costly.'

'You're saturated in capitalist dogma, Dice. You're clever, but you're just a tool of the fascist ruling class.'

They mounted the ridge. The path led down beside a low hill to their right, on to an exposed area of neatly cut grass many acres in extent broken only by the occasional tree.

'Drive on to the grass, right out into the middle, then pull up.'

'Killing Pope will not stop the Christian Democrats, nor will it advance world socialism, probably the reverse,' Dice said.

He did not add Carpenter's name to Pope's. But he knew that barring a miracle, Carpenter was already as good as dead. He had fully understood what the girl meant when she had said that she had already won. She had Carpenter under her rifle.

'It's not personal,' the girl said. 'Pope and Carpenter are representative of a fascist plot to subvert the working classes, put them under the yoke of religion to deliver them to the capitalist bosses. You call that freedom?'

'I wouldn't kill somebody just because they did not agree with me. But obviously you don't think the individual counts for much.'

'The individual must be subject to the common will. Stop here.'

Dice stopped the car, switched off the engine. They were in the very centre of the Heath. Apart from the odd tree, there was no cover for 400 yards in any direction. It was now full light.

So this was it. Whatever the terrorists expected to happen, it would happen here. But it might not occur. The arrest of Pina and the closure of the I.W.B. headquarters might have sent the entire organization into hiding. In that case he had to keep them talking, try to talk them past the crisis point when they realized that help would not arrive, when they were most likely to carry out their threat to detonate the bomb.

Dice had no high hopes of success. The fanatic, faced with failure, reacts invariably with insane violence.

The girl was looking at her watch. There was only one possible answer in view of the spot they had chosen. Crazy as it might seem in the centre of London, they were expecting an aircraft.

'I suppose the fact that Pope was black helped,' Dice said.

'What d'you mean?'

'Just another nigger.'

'Typical racist view. We don't make distinctions by colours.'

'You'd kill anybody, black, white, brown or yellow.'

'Shut up, Dice. You've talked enough.'

'You know the Russian word "chernozhopy"? It's the equivalent of "nigger", literally translated it means "black ass".'

The girl jammed the rifle into his neck. Her face, her eyes, stony.

'Don't preach to me, just don't.'

'I was trying to make a serious point. You have killed Alexander Pope. The Christian Democrats now have a martyr. Better still they have a black martyr. How will *that* go down in the third world?'

Unexpectedly, the girl relaxed, even permitted a slight, hard smile.

'You're good, Dice. You almost had me going then.'

'I mean it. The Western press will have a field day. Your political masters don't like individual actions like yours. Even if you get away, your reception might not be exactly what you expect.'

'That's my problem. Now be quiet. I want to listen.'

'I doubt . . .'

'I said BE QUIET!'

Dice looked away from her. He had done what he could. Now it was in God's hands.

61 Corelli stopped his car at the ridge, got out and stood staring at the stationary vehicle on the heath ahead.

It was immediately obvious that he could get no nearer without advertising his presence. Having heard the conversation in Dice's car, he was more aware than ever of the dangers of ill-considered or premature action. Like Dice, he still did not believe that a rescue attempt was a probability, and he knew from the conversation he had overheard what the outcome would be when the terrorists realized that they had no hope of escape. He did not expect that any of the occupants of Dice's car would live through the coming day. He swore softly but violently to himself, venting his bitter frustration.

The S.A.S. Lieutenant appeared beside him. The back-up

group had arrived, their vehicles drawn up behind his own under the lip of the ridge.

'What d'you think, Mr Bannister?' he asked.

Bannister looked out across the open space ahead of them, shook his head.

'I can deploy along this ridge, or I can split my men, put a party in position in compass points around the whole area. Whatever we do we cannot get within a quarter-mile of them, at least, not without risking being seen.'

'Then I think we'd better split your men up. We don't know what to expect, if anything. If there is trouble we're better off having them surrounded.'

'They're expecting an aircraft, aren't they?'

'I imagine so, nothing else I can think of would lead them to select this spot.'

'We only have rifles. We could do with something heavier.'

'No time. You'd better get your men moving . . . and remember, no firing unless I personally say so.'

Bannister nodded, not taking offence, understanding that Corelli was acutely anxious. He would have felt the same if one of his brother officers were out there.

Corelli went back to his car. There was no sound from the bug. Either it had been discovered or the girl was still maintaining silence. Silence whilst she listened. Listened for the aircraft, presumably.

Then he heard the distant noise, unidentifiable at first. Instinct alone told him the noise had relevance.

62 Dice heard the distant drone, then the dull *chop*, *chop*, *chop*, of the helicopter blades. The girl grinned at him, at the dismay registered on his face.

'You were wrong, weren't you?' she said.

Dice said nothing.

'You and the girl stay in the car,' she ordered. 'Carpenter comes with us. If you get out of the car, he dies.'

The helicopter was in sight now, coming in low over the ridge that hid Corelli and the back-up force. The pilot must have seen them.

The girl got out of the car, helped the man pull Carpenter awkwardly out of the back seat. The man walked out into the open with Carpenter a pace in front of him. He had the bared wires of the bomb in one hand, his Kalashnikov rifle in the other. The girl leant into the car, unable to resist a final word.

'I could kill you, Dice, you and the girl. But we don't kill for the sake of it, only because it's necessary, remember that.'

She did not wait for a reply but shucked her rifle from her shoulder into her hands and ran to catch up with the man and their prisoner.

The helicopter was hovering a few feet off the ground, perhaps fifty yards from the car. It was a two-seater; it might manage three, but certainly no more. They did not intend to take Carpenter with them. They would kill him before they took off.

Mary Tü scrambled up on to the back seat and stared out of the side window, tears streaming from her eyes and soaking into her gag.

Dice reached under his seat and took out an issue Walther automatic pistol. He was no more than an averagely competent shot, the range would be long, and he hated the very idea of killing, but he had no alternative.

He could not fire yet, nor could he call for help, not until the man let go of those wires. Dice was betting that they would not detonate the bomb for fear of damage to the helicopter, that they would leave Carpenter alone when they were within a few yards of the aircraft, then gun him down just before they took off. He would have a few seconds in which to kill them both and save Carpenter's life.

Dice released the safety catch on the Walther, wound down the passenger window and steadied the gun against the window frame.

The helicopter touched down.

* * *

63 Karelin kept the blades of the helicopter turning, he had no intention of being caught by the British police.

He picked up the skeletal bolt action rifle from the front seat beside him. It was his favourite weapon and, unlike Dice, he was a supremely accurate shot. It was an integral part of his business.

The terrorists were hurrying across the open grass towards him, the girl now leading, obscuring Carpenter and the man from his view. He had to take the man first, to prevent him detonating the bomb, but from Beida he had learnt that the girl was the more dangerous of the two.

Fifteen yards from the helicopter the man stopped Carpenter, left him standing like some grotesque scarecrow, swaying slightly, staggering a little to remain upright, and ran forward a few paces behind the girl.

Karelin fired. The magnum bullet struck the man on the bridge of his nose and was deflected the merest fraction before it smashed into his brain and out of the back of his head leaving a huge gaping exit wound. The force of the bullet stopped him as effectively as a brick wall, dropped him like a felled tree.

It took Karelin less than two seconds to work the bolt action and aim again, but the girl's reaction was even faster. She wasted no time trying to understand the inexplicable, ignored the helicopter, dropped to the ground, turning and firing as she fell, aiming for Carpenter, aiming to complete her mission.

Her bullets traced a bloody diagonal pattern across Carpenter's chest, knocked him backwards off his feet. As he fell, the bare wires touched and the bomb exploded, disintegrating the upper part of his torso, shattering the remainder of his body, scattering lumps of his flesh across the grass.

Karelin fired his second shot the instant the bomb exploded. It struck the girl behind her right ear, destroyed her face on exit.

Then Karelin dropped his gun beside him and powered the helicopter into the air, banking hard away to his right, away from the armed men behind the ridge, up and away across the rooftops of London.

* * *

64 Dice stood outside his car, watching the helicopter until it disappeared. Then he returned his gaze to the scene of carnage in front of him. The tension, the frustration had gone now, he felt only a deep sadness.

He untied Mary Tü's hands, ungagged her. Her body was limp, her eyes blank with horror. He sat her comfortably in the rear seat, but did not speak to her, she would not have heard.

A car came screaming across the grass towards them, skidded to a halt and Corelli scrambled out. He stopped in his tracks, staring at the dead bodies, at what remained of the Reverend Paul Carpenter.

'Bloody Hell! . . .'

Dice said nothing.

'The helicopter . . . I've sent a message back to warn the R.A.F. to try and intercept it,' Corelli said.

'The order will be cancelled higher up,' said Dice.

'What! Why . . .?'

'Politics.'

Corelli shook his head in bewilderment.

'I don't understand . . .'

'The pilot killed both the terrorists before I had a chance to fire. He tried to save Carpenter's life.'

'I know, I had binoculars on him, but . . .'

'Think, Ray. Who sent him?'

Corelli was silent for a moment, then enlightenment came.

'The K.G.B.?'

'Yes. They must have found the terrorists' British contact, then taken over the rescue operation. In their own highly individual way the K.G.B. were trying to save Carpenter.'

'Well, they bloody well failed.'

'So did we all. Even the terrorists. There's only one thing better than a dead martyr and that's two dead martyrs.'

Dice got into his car and started the engine. Mary Tü was slumped in the back seat, safe in that special internal fortress where the psyche retreats when assailed by traumatic shock. She sat motionless but for silent tears falling from vacuous eyes.

Dice drove away, towards the ridge, leaving Corelli staring after him.

65 Mary Tü regained consciousness in a hospital bed, the nightmare over, the nightmare yet to begin.

She was still heavy-headed from her drug-induced sleep but her brain was instantly clear, though she felt physically weak and carried, as she always would, a barely tolerable burden of sadness.

Dice entered the room, stood by the single bed, looking down at her.

'They said I could see you.'

She nodded.

'We will have to interview you, ask a lot of questions, but that can wait. For now, just one question. Do you mind?'

'No.'

It was the first time she had spoken aloud for three days. Her voice sounded strange, alien.

'Did Paul Carpenter speak to you, did he give you any instructions, tell you what was to happen if he died?'

He watched her anxiously.

'He said the time had come to move. We are to obtain maximum publicity for his death, put up candidates at every ward in the next election.'

'Then he knew they intended to kill him?'

'Yes, he knew. But he was not afraid.'

'He was a man of great faith.'

'Yes.'

There was a moment of shared silence before Mary spoke again.

'Mr Dice, I need a telephone. Would you ask them to bring a telephone in here?'

66 'Very messy business, Leonid,' said Firth.

'Yes. Regrettably so.'

They were in the bar of the Olivier Theatre on the South

Bank. It was the interval. Firth had originally suspected Maztikyan of irony when he saw the programme. They had watched the first act of *Much Ado About Nothing*.

Firth had ambivalent feelings about Shakespeare. The man was bawdy enough at times but too often obscure. Firth liked his jokes coarse and plainly understandable. He was happier here in the bar.

'The man who owns the helicopter was highly incensed,' he said.

'He had it safely returned.'

'He's sent the Commissioner of Police a bill for having it transported from Essex back to Kent. Karelin might have taken it a bit nearer the airfield he stole it from.'

'Borrowed.'

'As you wish. Very inconsiderate of him.'

'I should think he was in a hurry.'

'Probably. He rather botched the job, didn't he?'

'I gather not. An unfortunate accident. If Carpenter had fallen the other way . . .'

'Perhaps, but my masters are not pleased. Not at all pleased.'

'As I understand it you might have new masters within the year.'

'True,' said Firth, brightening, 'very true.'

A bell sounded.

'Ah,' said Maztikyan, 'the second act.'

67 'The body of Christ . . .'

The priest passed on down the line of communicants, placing the wafer tokens in their hands.

Dice had never been to this church before, had stopped there on his way to an empty home when he had seen that it offered an evening communion service.

He felt a need to thank God for Paul Carpenter's sacrifice, for the hope his death had brought to a world devastated by irreligious politics; he felt a need to restate his faith, to participate in the symbolic remembrance of that older sacrifice, that greatest of all acts of atonement.

'The blood of Christ . . .'

And the priest, unaware of this communicant's special need, held the cup to the lips of Allan Dice, policeman, kneeling thankfully at the communion rail.